THE LITERATURE OF
DEATH AND DYING

This is a volume in the Arno Press collection

THE LITERATURE OF
DEATH AND DYING

Advisory Editor
Robert Kastenbaum

Editorial Board
Gordon Geddes
Gerald J. Gruman
Michael Andrew Simpson

*See last pages of this volume
for a complete list of titles*

THE RESURRECTION
OF THE DEAD

by

KARL BARTH

Translated by

H. J. STENNING

ARNO PRESS

A New York Times Company

New York / 1977

Reprint Edition 1977 by Arno Press Inc.

Copyright 1933 by Fleming H. Revell Company
Copyright © renewed 1961 by
Hodder & Stoughton Ltd.

Reprinted by permission of
Hodder & Stoughton Ltd.

THE LITERATURE OF DEATH AND DYING
ISBN for complete set: 0-405-09550-3
See last pages of this volume for titles.

Manufactured in the United States of America

————◆————

Library of Congress Cataloging in Publication Data

Barth, Karl, 1886-1968.
    The resurrection of the dead.

    (The Literature of death and dying)
    Translation of Die auferstehung der toten.
    Reprint of the ed. published by Revell, New York.
    1. Bible. N. T. 1 Corinthians XV--Commentaries.
2. Resurrection. 3. Jesus Christ--Resurrection.
I. Title. II. Series.
BS2675.B32 1977   227'.2'06   76-19559
ISBN 0-405-09555-4

THE RESURRECTION
OF THE DEAD

by

KARL BARTH

Translated by

H. J. STENNING

NEW YORK

Fleming H. Revell Company

LONDON AND EDINBURGH

New York: 158 Fifth Avenue
London: 21 Paternoster Square

FOREWORD

THE chapter devoted to the Resurrection of the Dead does not stand in so isolated a relation to the First Epistle to the Corinthians as at first glance might appear. It forms not only the close and crown of the whole Epistle, but also provides the clue to its meaning, from which place light is shed on the whole, and it becomes intelligible, not outwardly, but inwardly, as a unity. We might even say that this *central* significance of the ideas expressed in the chapter extends beyond the limits of the First Epistle to the Corinthians. Here Paul discloses generally his focus, his background, and his assumptions with a definiteness he but seldom uses elsewhere, and with a particularity which he has not done in his other Epistles as known to us. The Epistles to the Romans, the Philippians, and the Colossians cannot even be understood, unless we keep in mind the sharp accentuation which their contents receive in the light of 1 Cor. xv., where Paul develops what elsewhere he only indicates and outlines, and which first imparts a specific and unmistakable colour to his ideas in general. How vitally important is the chapter, if this be the case, for understanding the testimony of the New Testament generally, I need not emphasize. That it is both right and necessary to subject it to an unusually detailed treatment seems to me to be obvious.

According to the usual conception, 1 Cor. xv. is
the last fragment in the great conglomerate of ex-
hortations, rebukes, and doctrinal pronouncements,
partly spontaneous, partly prompted by inquiries
from the Corinthian community, which, arranged
externally according to the needs and inspirations of
the moment, constitute together the so-called First
Epistle to the Corinthians. After Paul has replied
to the manifold questions of the Corinthian community, which provoked his intervention, he comes
at length to dwell upon the controversies agitating
Corinth with respect to the resurrection, and thus to
the resurrection itself. "Without internal or external
connexion with what has been said before, the treatment of a new theme then follows" (Lietzmann).
Such is the usual interpretation. It has the appearance of being self-evident. The haphazard character of the series of *subjects* dealt with in 1 Cor.
i.-xiv. is not to be disputed, nor is the lack of connexion by which 1 Cor. xv., with its new theme, is at
first joined to this series. But the question arises:
first, whether Paul's *reflections* upon the subjects
dealt with in 1 Cor. i.-xiv. are as disparate as these
subjects themselves, or rather whether a thread cannot be discovered which binds them internally into a
whole; and, secondly, whether 1 Cor. xv. is merely
to be comprehended as one theme by the side of
many others, or rather whether the thread hitherto
followed does not at this point become visible, so
that this theme, however much externally it is one
theme by the side of many others, fails to be recognized at the same time as the Theme of the Epistle.
It goes without saying that these questions are of

fundamental importance to the interpretation of 1 Cor. xv. If they are to be answered in the affirmative, we have before us in 1 Cor. i.-xiv., in fact the authentic commentary upon 1 Cor. xv. Consequently, in any attempt to answer them a detailed analysis of 1 Cor. i.-xiv. is indispensable.

"Though Christ offers us in the Gospel," says Calvin (Instit. ii. 9, 3), "a present plenitude of spiritual blessings, yet the enjoyment of them always lies hid under the custody of hope till we are divested of our corruptible body and transfigured into the glory of Him who is our first-fruits, our forerunner. In the meantime, the Spirit commands us to rely on the promises. Nor, indeed, have we otherwise any enjoyment of Christ any further than we embrace Him, as He is garbed in His promises. By which it comes to pass that *He Himself now dwells in our hearts* and yet we *live like pilgrims at a distance from Him,* because we walk by faith and not by sight."

JOHN CALVIN.

CONTENTS

The translator desires to acknowledge the valuable assistance which the Rev. R. Birch Hoyle has rendered in checking and revising this English version of *The Resurrection of the Dead.*

THE RESURRECTION
OF THE DEAD

I

THE TREND OF FIRST CORINTHIANS
I—XIV

§ 1

IN Corinth, Paul had to deal with an active and alert Church of a peculiar intellectual complexion. It was one of the first and probably the most important of the Christian Churches established upon pronounced Greek soil. Here the new religious matter, brought by the apostolic preaching, must have been accepted with passion, and, although not immediately assimilated, was yet absorbed in large understood-misunderstood lumps, and made available for that Church's own needs. The preponderantly proletarian composition of the Church was no obstacle to its participation in a philosophic-theological, cultic and ethical interest, of the intensity of which we can scarcely form an approximate idea. The force with which religious vitality was flowing through the new river-bed we may again divine from the opening words of the Epistle, where Paul testified that the Corinthian Christians have been enriched by God's grace (i. 5) in all utterance and all knowledge, in gifts and extraordinary capacities of every kind. But then a corrective is gently

13

applied. The testimony of Christ is indeed confirmed
in them (i. 7), a standard planted in a captured
position; but their own confirming, *in contrast* to
their enrichment, is placed in the future (i. 8): it
is because *God is faithful* that Paul really gives
thanks in these opening words (i. 9; cf. i. 4).
Clearly, Paul's intention is to bring them to their
senses, to provoke reflection, a reflection which is
designed to lift the eyes above the subjective gifts
of the Corinthian Christians to the Giver of all these
good things: utterance and knowledge and spiritual
gifts are to him manifestly no ends in themselves,
religious vitality itself no guarantee for Christian
severity that, blameless, awaits the end (i. 7-8).

NB

The idea that Paul wants to explain and bring
home to the Church founded by his gospel finds
direct expression in the long, coherent section,
(i. 10–iv. 21), which was evoked by the existence and
activity of three, perhaps four, different religious
groups, schools, or movements (schisms) constituting
the Corinthian Christians. In his observations upon
this fact, Paul makes hardly more than a few allu-
sions to the actual character of the ideas represented
by these movements; although one of the schools
of thought expressly carried on its agitation under
the flag of his own name, and although under the
name of Apollos, and probably also under that of
Peter, ideas were put forward which could not fail
to challenge him most sharply. It was far from his
thoughts to rush in helpfully to the assistance of this,
his own party, in its controversies with others; or to
intervene as arbitrator and peacemaker between it
and those which called themselves after Apollos and

Peter (i. 12). In his view, the question as to which amongst these groups was relatively most right, and the other question as to how the disputants could be reconciled, were manifestly quite secondary in comparison with the need for making all of them realize that it was not meet that the testimony of Christ set up among them, in contrast to the phenomena of the variegated religious fair, in the midst of which the Church life of the Corinthian Christians was lived, should be made into a cause, an idea, a programme, an occasion for intellectual exuberance and spiritual heroics, as this obviously is the essence of all religious movements and schools of thought, however excellent their intentions and deep rooted their foundations. The main defect of Corinthian conditions, from this point of view, Paul sees to consist in the boldness, assurance, and enthusiasm with which they believe, not in God, but in their own belief in God and in particular leaders and heroes; in the fact that they confuse belief with specific human experiences, convictions, trends of thought and theories—the special human content of which logically makes the recollection of particular human names unavoidable. In Corinth the testimony of Christ is threatening to become an object of energetic human activity, a vehicle of real human needs. Against this, the clarion call of Paul rings out: "Let no man glory in men" (iii. 21), or, expressed in positive form: "He that glorieth, let him glory in the Lord" (i. 31). "We preach Christ, who is the power of *God* and the Wisdom of *God* unto them that are called" (i. 24). Judge nothing before the time, i.e. do not be hasty in pronouncing final judgments upon the worth or worthlessness of your own and all other human experiences and motives, by your own too resolute decisions; for "every man shall have praise of God" (iv. 5). This "of God" is clearly the secret nerve of this whole (and perhaps not only this) section. The truth and the worth of the testimony of Christ lie in what in them *happens* to the man, happens from God; not what he is as man, nor what he makes of it, not in the word or the "gnosis" in man's acceptance of it. "The Kingdom of God is not in word" (generally understood: not in the subjective constitution of man) "but in power" (I interpret: to be and abide in the freedom of God the Lord) (iv. 20). "For other foundation can no man lay than that which is laid, which is Jesus Christ" (iii. 11). God always remains the *subject* in the relationship created by this testimony. He is not transformed into the object, into man's having the right to the last word: otherwise it is no longer *this* testimony, *this* relationship. "For who maketh thee to differ? and what hast thou that thou didst not receive? but if thou didst receive it, why dost thou glory, as if thou hadst not received it?" (iv. 7). "Was Paul crucified for you? or were ye baptized in the name of Paul?" he inquires (i. 13) of his own admirers. Do not your own words—I am of Paul! I am of Apollos!—show that you are yet carnal and walk after the manner of men, and have not yet grasped who has made you what you are? What is Apollos? What is Paul? (iii. 3-5). What, indeed, can men be, with their names, standpoints, and partisan outlooks? Ministers at best, through whose testimony belief is awakened, each according

to the special gift given him by the common Lord!
answers Paul (iii. 5). For we are *God's* fellow-
workers (iii. 9; the emphasis is on the first, and not
on the second word, as is the recent fashion of interpretation). Ministers of Christ and stewards of
the mysteries of *God* (iv. 1), and you, who think
you may or must swear by our name, you are God's
husbandry, God's building (iii. 9), the temple of the
holy God, which, for the latter's sake alone holy,
may not be defiled by over-weening self-deception
(iii. 16-17). We men may plant and water, but
"God giveth the increase" (iii. 6-7), and the fire of
judgment, wherein will be made manifest what our
work is worth or not worth, will pass over us all
without exception; and we must make up our minds
to see the whole of our work perish, rejoicing to
escape this fire ourselves: to be saved, not because
of, but in spite of, the work in which we took such
pride (iii. 12-15). Paul therefore withstood the
Corinthian factions: they take God for their own,
His right of judgment, His honour, His freedom.
You do not belong to, you are not in the service of
Paul, Apollos, or Peter: on the contrary, everything
is yours in Christ, is at your feet, at your service, is
your property—the world, life, death, present and
future, all are yours, and ye are Christ's and Christ
is God's! (iii. 21-23). You could and should accept
our testimony, the burden of which is man's direct
relationship to God, gratefully dismissing the witness
after he has rendered God's service to you, giving
God Himself the honour! And now Paul does not
dismiss as just modesty and humility, as the expression of a natural and justifiable need of assistance,

the fact that the Corinthians make no use of this
"All is yours!" of this sovereignty over all human
leaders and followers, but deliberately range themselves under this or that flag. He condemns this proceeding, *not* as a proof of their weakness, but as an
expression of the puffed-up egoism and consciousness
of strength of the *homo religiosus,* albeit under the
sun of Christian grace. With such religious movements, with such cultus of human programmes and
names, one is apt to puff himself up, in a spirit far
removed from real humility, against others who do
not belong to the school or the clique (iv. 6), "that
no one of you be puffed up for one against another."
The point he is making here is that they no longer
realize that all they are and all they have has been received from *God;* that they feel full, rich, masters—
in striking contrast to the feelings of him to whom
they were appealing. Paul adds: "I would like to
king it as you do!" (iv. 8). Strange inversion: while
you are enthusing and intoxicating yourselves, and
growing heated about what you have received from
us, we ourselves, the messengers and bearers, stand
there as the last, as those appointed to death, a spec-
tacle for the world, for angels and men; fools for
Christ's sake; whereas you are wise in that same
Christ, knowing everything so much better; strong
where we are weak, honoured where we are despised
. . . we scapegoats for the whole world, an offscour-
ing of all! (iv. 9-13). *Such* are the religious individuals in whose admiration and under whose flag
the Corinthians have made such splendid headway
that they have forgotten to fear God, and have thus
lost that which these individuals in reality brought

them! The warning which closes this train of thought is comparatively simple; it runs: Turn over a new leaf, return to the cause, to *God's* cause now, to the origin of your Christianity, to your begetting in Christ, which Paul might claim as his own achievement, though "ten thousand instructors" have passed over them. As a summons to return to Paulinism this would be a denial of all that has been said above: it is, however, a return to Paulinism only in so far as the last fragment of Paulinism consists in its own abnegation and suppression. "Wherefore, I beseech you, be ye followers of me" (iv. 16). The context makes this unmistakably clear: Come down from your wisdom, from your self-content, from your wealth, from the kingly consciousness which now fills you as Christians; come down from the brilliance of the all too Greek Christianity into which you have strayed, and, if you want to sail under the Pauline flag, come down into the foolishness and ignominy of Christ, where the truth is, where not man, not even the Christian man, but God is great, and where I, Paul, your father in Christ, am to be found.

The fundamental significance of this remarkable harangue, which I have substantially reproduced as it appears in chapters iii. and iv., emerges mainly from chapters i. and ii., to which we must therefore revert. Here Paul sets out the theoretical assumption on which his exhortation is based. It is not meet that the testimony of Christ should be made an object of religious athleticism and brilliance, as the Greek religious world was fond of doing, regarding in an all too human manner the Great, the Estimable, the Amazing simply in the relation of Either-Or. Paul said: It is simply the relationship of foolishness to wisdom, the wisdom of *God,* which is not as the wisdom of a man. He who with the Greeks seeks wisdom, his own wisdom, which he can inscribe upon a banner, with which he can posture, with which he can dogmatize, with which he can acquire something, such an one is as much astray as if, like the Jews, he had sought after the visible signs of the advent of the Son of Man. He finds only foolishness, nothing but sheer unintelligibility, just as the other, the Jew, finds here nothing but disgust and disappointment at the manifest absence of signs of majestic splendour (i. 22-23). Even as is God's wisdom, so too is the testimony of Christ shrouded in complete obscurity, and eludes any clumsy attempt to apprehend or comprehend it. It is the word of the Cross (i. 18), of salvation, that is only of God, that can only come to us from God, and ever and always comes from God alone. So are things placed in the scales in the Cross of Christ, which is the focus of the testimony of Him; on the one side, death is the last, the absolute last which we can see and understand; on the other side is life, of which we know nothing at all, which we can only comprehend as the life of *God* Himself, without having in our hands anything more than an empty conception thereof—apart from the fullness that God alone gives and His revelation in the resurrection. But in this section Paul, assuredly of set purpose, is not yet speaking of the resurrection. He intends here to enforce the preaching of the Cross against the religious vivacity of the Corinthians in its remorseless negativeness as the insoluble paradox,

as the angel with the flaming sword in front of the
shut gates of Paradise. Incisively he says (i. 17)
that to preach the gospel with wisdom of words (perhaps it would be nearer the meaning to translate this
"wisdom of life") is to make the Cross of Christ
void; when he declares (i. 18) that the power of
God, the royal freedom of God, which creates and
gives salvation to the saved, can only be foolishness
in the eyes of those who are perishing; that God de-
stroys the wisdom of the wise and brings to naught
the understanding of the prudent; when he inquires
almost ironically: "Where is the wise? where is the
scribe? where is the disputer of this world? hath not
God made foolish the wisdom of this world?"
(i. 20); when he says that, according to the wisdom
of God, the world with its wisdom could not know
God (i. 21). As exclusively as this is the salvation
which the gospel of Christ testifies to be understood
as God's salvation. The seriousness which charac-
terizes the Christian relationship to God is that the
things between God and man are of this nature.
Perhaps the Corinthians, in spite of their acknowledged wealth in utterance and knowledge and gifts,
or perhaps just because they are all too rich in these
things, have not yet grasped this seriousness. The
somewhat more positive things that Paul goes on to
say are, at any rate, not designed to create a speedy
reassurance here. He has already (i. 18) left it in
no doubt: the word of the Cross is God's power to
save, but, but—the word of the *Cross,* none other, is
foolishness, only foolishness to the lost. He then
says (i. 21) that it is, indeed, God's pleasure to save
them that believe, but through *that* in the preaching

which can only appear as wrong-headedness to them
that believe not. To believe, therefore, means absolutely to believe this *wrong-headedness,* and to
preach is to preach the *crucified* Christ, and the
Jews and Greeks *who are called* are those who, where
they, in the capacity of Jews and Greeks, can only
find a stumbling-block and foolishness, are not
vouchsafed a higher or deeper insight, but meet
Christ, *God's* power, *God's* wisdom (i. 22-25). It is
a very small consolation, as soon as we attempt to
ponder over these reflections as spectators and out-
siders—and all of us here are spectators and out-
siders, and always must be—to find Paul continuing
(i. 25): The *foolishness* of God—the only thing that
we of ourselves can grasp about God: that in Him
our thoughts are confounded, become foolishness
(and that not only by reason of our own incapacity,
but also through God's will and ordinance, i. 21)—
that is wiser than man; God's *weakness* (the disquieting void, into which God plunges us when the
Cross really becomes the criterion of knowledge of
God), *that* is stronger than man. Where are we
then? Where is there room for us between heaven
and earth? What then means salvation?

And then Paul illustrates this need—we can hardly
call it anything else—by what has been already mentioned as regards the mainly proletarian composition
of the Church. He uses it as a simile for the paradox
of Christian selection, upon which, in fact, their
Christianity is based, and which yet so threateningly
calls into question the vitality, the sweep, and the
élan with which they cultivate and nourish their
Christianity: the chosen are, indeed, always the

most foolish in the world—the weak, the base, the despised of the world—to shame the wise, to shame the strong. God has chosen—states i. 28, in philosophizing vein—the things that are not, to bring to naught the things that are. And all this (i. 29) so "that no flesh should glory in His presence." Of this God, however—that is, of the God who has chosen the things that are not—*are you;* you have your being in Jesus Christ (so Weizsäcker), who was made unto you wisdom from God, and righteousness, and sanctification, and redemption, in which only the Lord can be glorified (i. 30-31). This is now, indeed, the fullness, the positive, the creative force, which has made the Corinthian Christians. But it is not the fullness of their possessions; utterance, knowledge of God, and spiritual gifts are undoubtedly not referred to here, but the fullness of revelation, the wisdom in God's foolishness, the strength in God's weakness, the fullness in vacant space, which cannot be filled except by the reality, by the real speech and action of God Himself. The real speech and action of God at this place is the burden of the testimony of Christ, which has been established among the Corinthians. Paul wants to lead them back to this point, in order to see them confirmed.

NB

The second illustration of this hopeful need (ii. 1-5) is the recalling of Paul's own preaching, which was once the instrument of the call that came to the Corinthians. What happened then? Wisdom? Eloquent words, persuasive words? Nothing of the sort; on the contrary, on his part there was weakness, fear, and trembling. An impressive apostle as such would be no apostle. A winsome testimony would as such be no Christian testimony. The impressive and the persuasive may in its own sphere be necessary and right: from the apostle and his testimony it must always be, so to speak, subtracted: *beyond* this *his* greatness, there, where in his own name and by his commission he has nothing more to say; there, the Christly begins, the testimony of Christ the crucified on the side of the speaker, and the faith which is not man's wisdom but God's power on the part of the listener, the demonstration of the Spirit and of power (ii. 4-5). With any other argument than this, against which there is no appeal, Paul would have had no reason to have come to Corinth at all. Whatsoever does not grow from the soil of this argument is, the Corinthians must be made to realize, not the legitimate continuation of the Christianity evoked by his preaching. And now the conclusion of the second chapter (6-16) carries this fundamental conception to its highest point. The wisdom we refer to when we speak of righteousness, sanctification, redemption, is wisdom for the perfect, the wisdom and mystery that is hidden (ii. 6-7). But be it clearly understood: Man does not attain to this wisdom through the pursuit of some esoteric knowledge and the like. Nor is it reached by some such way as that of Christian speculation, and the "perfect" who possess it are not to be sought in the higher world of spirits and devils, the rulers of this world. Therefore, according to Paul, even the so-called dæmoniacal is not some kind of organ for revelation. It is a question of the wisdom of God. In its pres-

ence the lower human as well as the higher dæmoniacal world fail; and it avails us little if, as men,
we should happen to stumble upon their knowledge.
By rejecting and crucifying Christ, the highest and
best world-powers just proved their blindness for
God. But: "Eye hath not seen, nor ear heard,
neither have entered into the heart of man, the things
which God hath prepared for them that love Him!"
quotes Paul from an unknown source (ii. 9). Only
God Himself can be the subject of the knowledge of
God: The Spirit which God gives, and which, as the
Spirit of God, searcheth the "deep things" of God,
which it alone can know (ii. 10-11). As those who
had received the *Spirit* of *God*, we know what is sent
us from God in Christ the crucified. As such and to
such we also speak. All speaking and listening in the
Christian Church is based upon the assumption of
the divine, holy Spirit, which opens here the mouth,
there the ears. The third thing excluded, however,
is wisdom, about which not Spirit with spirit, but
man with other men, converse. Paul complains
movingly (iii. 1-2) that he had obviously not yet
succeeded in speaking to them in the Spirit, and in
being understood by them in the Spirit. As carnal,
as babes in Christ, he fed them with milk and not
with meat, not with a pædagogic intention, as this
passage is usually but quite absurdly and incoher-
ently interpreted, but because they, the Corinthians,
were not yet able to hear his word as the word of
God. The words in question mean, "I have not
managed." It was not the intention, but the melancholy consequence, that he gave them milk instead
of meat, because most regrettably they thought they

were going to hear expositions of "human wisdom," a new philosophy or theology, whereas Paul was concerned with the testimony of God's self-revelation. A Christian pneumatologist would be a man who, in contrast to the things which they prized and cultivated, "has the mind of Christ" (ii. 16), the knowledge of which God is not only object but also subject. Therefore they would not be able to digest this meat with which he, Paul, had once actually fed them. Their incapacity (iii. 2) transformed the wisdom of *God* which was offered them into wisdom of *man*. That this was still true of them is shown by the partisanship of which the third and fourth chapters speak. This is the profoundly insufficient and unsatisfactory character of their situation, which Paul, in acknowledging all that has to be acknowledged, above all reveals, and out of which he wants to help them. What Christianity is specially concerned about is Christian knowledge; not about this and that, about things, even though they be the last things, but about the Either-Or, the understanding or the failure to understand the three words *apo tou theou* (from God). Unless everything deceives, that is the trend of Paul's utterance (1 Cor. i.-iv). Are not position and counter-position in the conflict about the resurrection, which 1 Cor. xv. will disclose, already visible here in outline?

§ 2

We will now turn first to chapters v. and vi., which have this in common, that Paul's criticism levelled at Corinthian Christianity assumes a predominantly

ethical character. Here, in contrast to the preceding
section, the practical paranese comes first (v. 1-6)
and the basic viewpoints follow (vi. 12-20), although
prepared by important elucidations (v. 6-13 and
vi. 8-11). Two concrete *occasions* prompt Paul's
complaints. The first is the fact that the community
has allowed one of its members to contract a marriage, inadmissible even according to pagan sentiment and Roman law (v. 1). The other is the fact
that the community is not shocked at its members'
appealing to pagan judges in cases of legal dispute
(vi. 1). The treatment of both cases is entirely
similar. Both, in his view, signify a regrettable lapse
on the part of the Corinthians. "Know ye not," is
asked again and again (v. 6; vi. 2, 9, 15, 16, 19).
An urgent reminder of assumptions that should go
without saying is the tenor of the whole section. It
has been forgotten that there is one kind of development of human vitality which in the Christian
Churches, here only, but here absolutely, is forbidden
and excluded; that the Church is sick if it does not
react against such egoistic exuberance of man in its
midst, however natural and understandable it otherwise is, however little surprised one may be to see it
everywhere occurring. We are not concerned here
with the pride of the religious man, as in chapters
i.-iv., but we find ourselves several stages lower, in
the sphere of sexuality and of the impulses of *phys-
ical* life (vi. 3), the *meum* and *tuum* interests of the
self-same man. But with all their variety, all these
things are, from Paul's standpoint, fundamentally
on one and the same level; the manner in which,
in v., he refers directly to the incestuous person in

speaking of those who find the Kingdom of God in the word of man (iv. 20), is a plain indication in this respect. Here as there, we are concerned with the same thing: chapters i. to iv. are *also* to be understood in an ethical sense, and what is complained of in chapters v. and vi. is *also* a lack of knowledge. Here as there, it has been forgotten by the Corinthians that the Christian Church in relation to Logos *and* Ethos is the crisis of the natural, savage man and his higher or lower spiritual vitality. It *is* that. Paul speaks of it not in the imperative or the optative but in the *indicative* mood. On the plane of the Christian Church, there is an altogether other, a new thing. "Ye are 'unleavened,' " we read in v. 7, with allusion to the Old Testament injunction, that at Passover time not only might no leavened bread be eaten, but no leaven was allowed to exist at all. Ye are unleavened and our own paschal lamb is slain: Christ. And still more distinct and partly without imagery (vi. 11): "but ye are washed, but ye are sanctified, but ye are justified in the name of the Lord Jesus, and by the Spirit of our God." (Note the "but" twice repeated with which this assertion is categorically detached from what has preceded it.) This other new thing, which is here asserted is, according to Paul, an unheard-of, boundless promise under which the Church is placed. Nor should this positive side of the matter be here overlooked. Let us keep the feast . . . with the unleavened bread of "sincerity and truth," he also exclaims in the essentially more sharply pointed chapter v. (verse 8), with a suppressed joy. "Awake, Easter Day is here!" And the viewpoint from which

he immediately opens the discussion of the lawsuit
question (vi. 2) is, if possible, even bolder and more
joyful. Christians, as such, are not only, as ii. 15
prescribes, fundamentally in the *position*, but are
called, to judge the world, and even the angels, to
test and distinguish spirits, to recognize and pro-
nounce the last clearest truth. But this high
promise, as such, is at the same time also the judgment under which the Church stands. In so far as it
is not realized in the Church, the latter is necessarily
open to accusations and judgments. But the Passover cannot be kept with the old leaven. The
unrighteous shall not inherit the Kingdom of God
(vi. 9). Be it observed that these accusations are
not directed in a moralizing way against the sins of
the world. v. 9-13, very distinctly asks what call
had he to judge them that were without. "Do not
ye judge them that are within" (v. 12). The majesty of the claim and the menace that are here set
up, is indeed hidden from those that are without;
just as, according to ii. 14, the hidden wisdom of
God is also utter foolishness to them. Therefore, we
are concerned with the new negation that is here
visible; hence not to criticize the world, nor to raise
oneself above it, not to distinguish Christians before
the heathen. Christians cannot and ought not to go
out of the world (v. 10). Consequently, the question is to enforce the right of *God*. That is what is
to happen in the *Christian Church*. That is the place
in the world (*in* the world) where the right of God,
and therefore accusation and judgment regarding the
wrong-doing of man, come to light. Be it further
noted, that this accusation also is not directed in

moralizing fashion against the individual who has transgressed. It is directed against the Church, as such, and runs: It—the Church—is not what it yet *is* in Christ! It does not know instinctively, that it must, not out of pharisaism, but simply as a matter of order while lamenting the necessity, cut off from its body such a member as the person guilty of incest (v. 2); not in order to anticipate God's judgment upon him with its own hands, but so that God's honour here in the flesh, so far as in it lies, will not be stained (v. 5). And it does not know instinctively that, without confusing heavenly and earthly things, it may not calmly look on while its members appeal to a right and a judgment which it, the Church, cannot recognize in their dignity and validity with all seriousness. Paul says it more sharply: those who are least esteemed! (vi. 4). Why does it not draw the strength out of its own resources to settle such disputes concerning "mine" and "thine." Why, indeed, have such disputes arisen among them at all? Why is it not preferred in such cases to suffer wrong than to do wrong? (vi. 7). To the accusation v. 3-5 is attached the express injunction, to deal with the guilty person in the manner prescribed. He, Paul, although absent in body, yet among them in the spirit, will himself execute the terrible act of purification, the delivery up of the rebel to Satan, who alone can save him. For only when judgment is executed upon the flesh can the spirit be saved in the day of judgment. The Church does not so much owe to itself as to its Master, and to that extent just to its unworthy and impossible members, to execute the Either-Or, not only by words, but by significant actions visible from afar.

In the second case, Paul gave no express injunction. But it will not for this reason be found that he expresses his opinion of what ought to be done in a less binding and urgent manner. Chapter vi. 12-20 develops the principle of this section in a special glance at the first case. It sounds as if he were answering an unspoken objection when in vi. 12 he again interposes with: "All things are lawful for me." This was, according to ii. 15; iii. 21; vi. 2, Paul's own preaching. Does this mean that the Christian, made lord of all things, has in Christ the right, and probably the duty, simply to be a man again like all other men, to assert his personality, to satisfy his instincts, to seek his right where he finds it? Manifestly as little as God can employ His omnipotence and freedom anywhere and anyhow to be no longer God. Paul gives first two provisional answers (vi. 12); he says first: "All things are not expedient," and then (to explain what he regards as inexpedient): "I will not be brought under the power of any." The limit of my power over all is exactly where I have power over things, the point where it is not transformed into power over me. Where that happens, and that is happening in Corinth, things have just gained power over men. What passes for freedom there, is in reality slavery. But this answer is only preparatory; the decisive is now to follow: Man in his earthly existence is not only belly, he not only vegetates, he is body; he is in and with his vegetating corporeality created by

God and destined for God. Is the belly corruptible;
is it subject for God's sake to the judgment of death,
then the body is due to the Lord, whom God raised
up, as He will also raise up us, our body, through
the power of this Lord (vi. 13-14). Our corporeality
as God's work and property (as such, to be sure,
here and now invisible) are members of the body of
the risen Christ, one Spirit with it. Fornication,
and all human *hybris,* however, signify that not only
our corruptible, but also our incorruptible part
is surrendered. Christ's members become in the
members of the harlot one flesh with Him (vi. 15-
17). That is the great impossibility of unbridled
human vitality, the dragging down into the dust not
only of man, but (Paul did not, according to 6-15,
shrink from this thought) of the *Lord,* His being
made captive by matter, by something earthly, by a
thing. The authority of God may not be threatened;
it is that to which our power must set iron barriers.
And it is threatened when man persists in thinking
that he is permitted to follow his vital impulses.
Christ's right over us and consequently Christ Himself are in that case subordinated to the world's
right. That Paul actually saw this danger of sexual
license in a specially revolting form, is from his "Flee
fornication" (vi. 18) very clear. But the quite
special accentuation of this remarkable passage unmistakably emphasizes what is fundamental: We are
in no sense to regard our earthly existence, our body,
as an opportunity to exhaust our vitality. We are
not our own masters. "Ye are not your own."
Rather are we dearly bought. We belong to Another. We have a Master. The Holy Ghost dwells

in us; we are His temple. To praise God with our
body and with our spirit is the purpose of our existence (vi. 19-20). Hence the protest and the demand
which Paul made (v. 1; vi. 11). It must be clear
how and to what extent this section with its peculiar
severity, with its occasional passages of mordant
incisiveness, especially at the end, is sensibly connected with the preceding one. The flaming sword,
"from God," which was *there* unsheathed as the
Christian truth against the religious velleities of the
Corinthians, is raised *here* accusingly and menac-
ingly over their natural life, in which they feel secure
or even strengthened by the Pauline "All things are
lawful for me." Christianity brings not peace but
unrest into the natural life; it transforms it into
the members of the body of the risen Lord, which,
as such, shall be sanctified. Against the life urge of
man, Paul opposes the unassailable truth that he
cannot do what he wants: the imperious question,
whether and how in his actions he will honour or
dishonour the Lord. A hand has been held out to
man which will not let him go. Paul does not pursue
this theme further. It is not an independent theme,
but a paradigm like the preceding. Again, from a
new angle, something has become visible in outline,
of what he will, in chapter xv., proclaim as the
Resurrection of the Dead.

§ 3

Chapter vii. constitutes a section by itself. An
unspoken question is in the air, just as in the immediately preceding case. If, then, man in Christ is

forbidden to expend his vitality; if the sphere of sexuality is that in which the danger is particularly great of his doing so; if, then, for the sake of God's honour, it is just here that we must remember the phrase "All things are lawful unto me" has its necessary inner limitation—must, then, the struggle against human wilfulness and presumption not also and perhaps mainly become a struggle against *all* sexuality, a struggle against marriage? For what distinguishes the captivity in which man and his heavenly Lord are involved through fornication from that which holds sway even in the orderly sexual relations of civic life? Is it worth while, then, when once the sanctity of the body created by God, and destined for God, its waiting for the resurrection, is known, to halt just at this point, and be indulgent? That was the question which was obviously more or less energetically denied by one of the many sections in the Corinthian Church. Sexual abstinence was recommended and practised in marriage according to vii. 3. According to vii. 12-13, marriages were dissolved where one of the partners was not Christian, and virginity was proclaimed (vii. 25 *et seq.*) as the Christian ideal. The all-embracing tolerance with which obviously the majority of the Church let things run their course was confronted by the rigorism of a radical-ethical group. We shall meet their traces again. In dealing with them Paul was not in an easy position; for there can be no doubt that, so far as he was concerned, he was in practical agreement with their trend of thought. He might perhaps repudiate and oppose their motives, their theology, but he could not say no, at least for himself, to the results of their deliberations. "It is good for a man not to touch a woman," he begins by saying in vii. 1. Temporary sexual abstinence in marriage seems to him advisable in order to gain time for prayer (vii. 3), and in the impossibility of entirely keeping it he sees plainly incontinence. To him, marriage is a divinely ordained condition only in so far as it is a means of avoiding adultery or "burning" (vii. 5; ix. 26). To refrain from divorcing an unbelieving wife he ventures to recommend as his own, not as the Lord's command (vii. 12). To marry is no sin, but whoever does so is inviting trouble, which Paul would gladly spare him (vii. 28). He that is married is forced to care for the things of the world, and how he may please his wife (vii. 33). He that marries does well; but he that marries not does better (vii. 38). Happier is a widow who does not marry again, in his opinion (vii. 40). And Paul's concluding words to this very last sentence run: "And I think also that I have the Spirit of God." All this betrays a fundamentally different sentiment from that which prompted Luther to describe the "sacred" state of marriage as a state and order altogether pleasing to God. No, here sexuality is manifestly under the heaviest shadow and suspicion, and Paul's personal opinion is that, in order to seek the honour of the Lord, it is better to remain single (vii. 31-35). Nevertheless, as an apostle, as a responsible witness of revelation, he did not say yes to the tendencies of that ascetic school. He contented himself by emphasizing through his public example all those injunctions to the married: "for the fashion of this world passeth away" (vii. 31). Moreover, if one is married, he can only be married as if he were not (vii. 29). A last remnant of freedom, a last glimmer of consciousness of being neither man nor woman, nor a sexual being, must also be kept alive in marriage as the retrieved recollection of the corruptibility which governs this life, if it is impossible to shape one's life entirely in the light of such a recollection. In so far as the chapter emphasizes *this* "inner-worldly" asceticism in its acutest form, it is to be regarded as a simple supplement to chapter vi. But in its main intention—and here Paul is writing formally against himself—it also designs to expound something else, namely: not a justification of marriage (which will be found here no more than a justification of the State in Rom. xiii.) but a warning against the *hybris* of sexual asceticism (just as Rom. xiii. is a warning against the *hybris* of revolution and nothing else).

Sexual abstinence or celibacy is, in Paul's view, a gift of God, a condition that is desirable, but only to be bestowed by God. *Above* his own well-founded opinion on this matter, and *against* the enthusiasm of those who made the matter into a principle, Paul also employs here the words "from God." So that not even the opposite of sensuality, not even asceticism, may be elevated into any principle that infringes God's sovereign right, into an intrinsic truth. "Circumcision is nothing, and uncircumcision is nothing, but the keeping of the commandments of God" (vii. 19). It is *God* who stands in the way of the *licentious*, but it is also *God* who stands in the way of the radical moralists. "Let every man,

wherein he is called, therein abide with God" (vii
24). "Let every man abide in the same calling
wherein he was called" (vii. 20). Can there be any
worse presumption than to disturb this order under
the pretext of designing to serve heaven? Regarded
from this side—we have thrown the other side into
strong relief—this chapter also falls into line. It
makes it clear that the severity of "from God" applies not only to the wicked, but also to the good and
the "unco guid"; that the meaning of the goal to
which the whole Epistle is moving is the glory of
God and really only the glory of God.

§ 4

The next perceptible unity is comprised in chapters viii.-x. The subject of which Paul speaks in
viii. 1, and to which he reverts in x. 25, is the dispute raging at Corinth around the question whether
and to what extent a Christian is permitted to eat
flesh that has been slaughtered for pagan sacrificial
purposes and subsequently sold in the market. An
emphatic negative was confronted by an equally
sweeping affirmative opinion and practice, the self-
consciousness reposing on the freedom of their
conscience of some, the irritated and wounded sus-
ceptibility of others. The practical counsel that
Paul gives is found in x. 25-28; its purport is not to
inquire over-anxiously into the origin of publicly or
privately offered food, but emphatically to reject it
once its origin from a heathen temple, without any
specific inquiry from others, has been established.
We are dealing with a certain meditated and note-

worthy proposal to discover some sort of a path
between freedom and constraint of conscience, or
the conscience *temporum ratione,* similar to the more
or less peremptory or cautious pastoral advice with
which we have become acquainted in chapters v.-vii.
But Paul did not write either chapters v.-vii. or
chapters viii.-x. for the sake of these practical injunctions. Each time the way is more important
than the goal, or rather the way, the real teaching
on which the imparting of these counsels is based, is
the real goal of this section. Thus here too, it is as
if Paul took a sponge and sponged out all the advice
he had just imparted, when he writes in x. 31,
"Whether therefore ye eat, or drink, or whatsoever
ye do, do all to the glory of *God.*" That is the goal
of this section.

The front upon which he fights in these three
chapters is directed altogether specially against his
own followers in the Church; for it can scarcely
be doubted that the conception to which he appeals
here as a warning and corrective was fundamentally
his own. We have seen how, in chapter vii. Paul
wrote to a certain extent against himself, against the
experiment of sexual abstinence embarked upon by
a few in Corinth, which, for his own person, he quite
unequivocally regarded as right. Here, in chapters
viii.-x., in the case of antagonism between a free
and a legally emasculated and solicitous Christianity,
Paul must feel much more concerned, and this time
far in excess of the mere personal equation. The
whole ninth chapter would be incomprehensible if
Paul had not obviously felt *at one* with the Corinthians who thought *freely* and *untrammelled* upon

this question. They were certainly not identical with the people who were in agreement with him regarding the subject dealt with in chapter vii. Paul, however, is the same person who *there* expressed as his own personal opinion the unambiguous sentiment: "It is better not to marry," and *here* the freedom of the Christian conscience from all pettiness and restriction. Independent, wilful, and regardless of the reproach of inconsistency, he plunges with his opinion, straight through the various camps into which the Church was split up, indifferent whether he appears now as an ascetic, now as a man of the world. He has his own programme and his own way. We do not know whether the ethical radicals of chapter vii. also appealed to his name; it may be. What is certain is that in chapter viii. he stepped into the camp of his own, the real Pauline, people. It is a question of freedom (ix. 1, 19; x. 29) of power (ix. 4, 12) to do or refrain from doing this or that; and x. 23 takes up again with due emphasis the theme of vi. 12: "All things are lawful." The question he is discussing is the freedom created in Christ, the power conferred upon him as an apostle, which Paul quotes in the ninth chapter as an analogy, and the whole Epistle to the Galatians testifies how vitally important this freedom was to him. We find in viii. 4-6 a short description of the fundamental standpoint which had been adopted by the Pauline Corinthians and approved by Paul himself. Their objection to the rigorous Christians in the matter of meat offered to idols was profound and fundamental; "an idol is nothing . . . and there is none other God

but one" (viii. 4). With the hypothetical, yes,
even with the real, existence of many gods and lords
in heaven and on earth, Paul is, indeed, quite prepared to reckon: "For though there be many that
are called gods," verse 8 expressly states. *But* viii.
6 majestically continues "but *to us* the *one* God the
Father, of whom all things, and we in Him; and one
Lord Jesus Christ, by whom all *things,* and we by
Him." It will be noted that the word "is" relating
to God and Christ is missing from this sentence in
the Greek. The gods exist: the one God, the Father,
does *not* "exist." In place of "to be" or any other
predicate he uses with proud satisfaction the word
hēmin—he is God "to us," and the character of His
relations to the world and to us is indicated by
the prepositions "of whom," "in whom," and "by
whom." This evinces an insight which is not less
important because, like the expression "things which
are not" (i. 28), it is clothed in philosophical language and was at least not alien in form to the
deeper conception of his Greek contemporaries. It
might very well have been that Paul used here the
language of his Greek followers rather than his own.
What remains valuable to us is that he was able to
say here what he wanted: the fundamental (like the
distinction between being and non-being) distinction between the gods and our God, the God, Father
and Lord, who has the power to command is: in the
world, in the world of existing things are the former:
the latter, the one revealed to us is the *origin,* the
Creator of all things. But what did Paul mean here?
He omitted to complete the antithesis. We can only
guess what he meant by the following: According to

viii. 7, there were in Corinth certain persons who had not yet broken away from familiarity with idols, although they were Christians. They had not yet grasped that shattering distinction between God and idols. They were still peering timidly into the world, at things existent, at the fact that idols, at least, exist; the words "to us there is but one God," although they even uttered them as a Christian confession, had not yet availed to depress the idols into the sphere of relativity, in which they, in spite of, nay, because of, their existence, must appear to be as nothings. They were still reckoning with them as with powers which could at least *compete* with God. The pagan-sacramental sphere was repugnant and dangerous to them, but must still be taken with religious severity, and, precisely because they continued to take them with religious severity, they appeared to them repugnant and dangerous. Hence the meat offered to idols was to them real meat offered to idols, repellent as such, and a serious matter. Their Christianity still consisted essentially in a convulsive tension between the regard fixed on God and the regard fixed on idols, between pure and impure, between pious and impious acts. To eat meat offered to idols would be for them a violent and illegitimate disturbance of the tension, an invasion, a relapse into the necessity of idols and lords, a stain on their consciences. Paul's attitude towards them is plain enough: the "familiarity with idols" is broken. The glance fixed on God, and the distinction between Him and the other gods, has wrought such a devastating effect that the glance fixed on the latter loses all significance; if they exist, they do not compete with God. The tension between them and God is so radical, that all struggle and convulsion can cease. They no longer even count in their relation to God; the pagan-sacra-mental sphere has ceased to be dangerous, because it is recognised as merely profane. There is *no* such thing as meat offered to idols; there is only ordinary meat. Why should it not be bought and eaten? Paul later indicates all this incidentally: "All things are lawful" (x. 23) only because, according to viii. 6, all things are from God the Father and all things are by the Lord Jesus Christ. The earth is the Lord's and the fullness thereof (x. 26); over Him the gods have no dominion. We can eat, drink, and do whatever else, all to the glory of God (x. 31), when we know, according to viii. 5, that we are created in Him and by Him, by the Lord Jesus Christ. This therefore is the real Pauline opinion about sacrifices to idols—his standpoint, so to speak; just as respecting the subject of chapter vii. his opinion was that it was better not only for him, but for everyone, not to marry than to marry, if that were possible. Nor has Paul, here, cheaply sur-rendered his own opinion upon the matter to another and more arresting consideration. Instead, he pro-ceeded first to support it in the ninth chapter by a rather far-reaching analogy: He, Paul, also knows what it is to do this or that for the sake of the self-consciousness and right of a free conscience through God. Towards the Corinthians, and in this case especially towards the strict among them, he feels with pride that he is, what no one else can be to them, the apostle (ix. 1-2). Appealing to this fact, and to the fact that he has seen the Lord (ix. 1), he proceeds to shatter all criticism of his attitude (ix. 3). He claims the right to do what he likes with regard to eating and drinking, and to found a family after the example of Peter and the brethren of Jesus (ix. 5-6). He claims, above all, the right to be supported by the community instead of earning his own livelihood (ix. 7). To the soldier his pay, to the vine-grower and the shepherd their share in the results of their labour, and "Thou shalt not muzzle the ox that treadeth out the corn!" In hope, i.e., not in vain, shall the ploughman plough and the thresher thresh as God has ordained (ix. 9-10). "If we have sown unto you spiritual *things, is it* a great *thing* if we shall reap your carnal *things*" (ix. 11). Just as, according to the law of the Old Testament, the priests and their assistants were permitted to partake of the sacrifice, so has the Lord ordained (Paul might have recollected Luke x. 7: "The labourer is worthy of his hire") that they who preach the gospel should live by the gospel (ix. 13-14). If he has made no use of this right to reward, no one at least is entitled to minimize the glory, the justifiable pride which he gains by way of reward for his voluntary activity—he seems to mean in the obscure, perhaps textually mutilated verse ix. 15. So far the *analogy* is intended to show the reader that Paul also knows the meaning of permission, freedom, having the right, having control of extensive and delightful worldly possibilities. But the meaning even of these three chapters is not just the continuous enforcement of the Pauline standpoint. The line which we have so far followed is strongly

intersected by another, and the latter remains
determinative and victorious. Stronger even than
in chapter vii. respecting his particular opinion of
marriage, it is here shown that even his doctrine of
freedom, however profound and intimately bound
up with his gospel, also has its limits; that an in-
flexible Pauline dogma does not exist so far as he,
its author, is concerned. This manifest, temporary
self-suppression, this subdual of Paul by Paul, this
shaking of his own standpoint to its very foundations
looking to the object of this standpoint, that is what
makes this chapter, after Rom. xiv.-xv., most particularly important and significant. The decisive
thing that Paul has to urge against himself and his
school transpires at once from the three first verses
of the section, viii. 1-3, where he calls knowledge
the proper standpoint from which to regard offering
meat to idols. We all of us have this proper standpoint, he says, somewhat ironically, perhaps quoting
a letter addressed to him. In verse 7 this pronouncement is supplemented and corrected by the other:
"not in every man is this knowledge." Here, in
verse 1, the fact that *all* have the gnosis, the
knowledge, contributes, at any rate, to place the
gnosis, despite its incontestable correctness, in a
somewhat fatal light immediately. A standpoint
that "we all" have is apt for this reason, whatever
its nature may be, to become a questionable thing.
"Knowledge puffeth up," he continues. How, it may
be asked: the opinion that there are no gods, the
opinion that there is no God but one? Yes, undoubtedly, precisely this opinion! This opinion, too, this
standpoint like every other (iv. 6, 19), Paul shows

here—that what he had to say generally in the first chapter about the religious sections in Corinth was inspired by a spirit of impartial severity. An unnatural and arrogant puffing up of men is everywhere apparent where an attempt is made to set up an opinion as true in itself, to enforce it, to assert it continuously, unmindful of its object. Not that in the least, even were it a thousand times truer! Precisely not a knowledge in itself! Not a firm and consistent knowledge that has become unshakable, not a gnosis that by virtue of its own gravity now stands square with the dignity of its own inner righteousness, and thus, in the last resort, for its own sake; not a mere belief that we possess knowledge (viii. 2), not an idea that on this point we have settled and finished and thought out the matter to the end. Else knowledge, this high and serious matter, were no longer knowledge, and whoever regards it as such has not yet understood, as he ought to, that word "Love edifieth" (viii. 1). The great theme of chapter xiii. appears here for the first time. A glance at viii. 3 shows that here at any rate we are concerned with the love of God. In this connexion love must at any rate mean devotion of the subject of knowledge to its object, objective reality instead of subjective, severity not towards one's own conviction (which would be the knowledge that puffeth up itself and can be no real knowledge), but severity of interest for that which, in one's own conviction, might perhaps appear to be really *against* it; severity of the gravity and dignity of truth, which resides not in man but in God, the severity of frankness and humility, in which God, the true God,

known as distinct from all other gods, rejoices less
to be understood as Object, than in *allowing* Himself to be understood as *Subject,* that *He* is right
and not man. This love (in knowledge) edifies, says
Paul. It is the positive element, the truth in all
knowledge. Where it is (viii. 3), man is known of
God, and God Himself enters as the positive element,
the truth in knowledge, and makes it, if not fertile
and creative, as we should doubtless like to see, yet
solid and significant, judicial and teeming with
imagery. *Cogitor, ergo sum,* "I am thought of,
therefore I am," it may mean then, and this *cogitari,*
this *"being* thought of," its logic, consistency, and
certitude will prevail over the knowing man, although, indeed, just because the *cogitare,* the *self-*
thinking, with its logic about it and from it, in new
and other newer forms can only come to naught,
even if our subjective knowing manifestly continues
to consist of a series of broken beginnings apparently
talking into the void. *God* is then true in this
cogitor, this "being thought-of" (by God), and all
men with their *cogitare,* with their *self-*thinking, are
liars. It is not difficult for us to recognize here in a
new shape the fundamental idea of the first section,
chapters i.-iv. especially the pneumatological doctrine of that vital sub-section ii. 6-16, except that
now it is even more distinct than there; that Paul
is not perhaps thinking of building his own theology
with his "from God" and defending it against the
other people, that he rather sees this flaming sword
turned against himself and those who march with
him as much as against anybody. The execution of
the "diastasis" between God and man, the discovery

of the unheard-of change of subject and object into
what is called Revelation, signifies for him not, as in
a well-known theological work of our time, the
criticism of this or that, but the crisis *of all* theology,
including the best, and including his own. From this
standpoint, therefore, from that of Love, or what is
the same thing, from the standpoint of the Knowledge of God, in which God is subject, he will now
set limits to his own bold, and to him so vitally
important, doctrine of freedom.

§ 5

We shall perhaps best follow him first in the
interim discussion of the ninth chapter, as the conclusion of the eighth chapter, verses 9-3, although
placed at the beginning, is actually nothing less than
the preparation for that confession (10, 25 *et seq.*)
which, apart from the concluding words, crowns the
whole. The discussion, in the ninth chapter, of
apostolic freedom, is first (ix. 12) abruptly interrupted by the sentence, "Nevertheless we have not
used this power!" He repeats himself at the com-
mencement of verse 15, and, after that somewhat
obscure intermediate sentence, in ix. 16, lays down
the foundation: the preaching of the gospel yields
me nothing, not even glory, let alone the reward
that might at least be reserved to a voluntary
worker. Constraint, necessity, is imposed on me:
woe to me if I do not preach the gospel! If I did it
on my own deliberation, I should expect a reward,
I should have the right to make use of that freedom:
but if I do it in despite of my own resolve, then I am

only entrusted with a dispensation (ix. 17). My reward consists in having no reward (ix. 18). That is the limitation which Paul sees drawn around him as an apostle. He hears himself called to do what he (vi. 19) calls upon others: "Ye are not your own." Thou livest not in thine own business: thou dost not bear the tidings, but the tidings bear thee; it does not need thee, but thou needest it; here thou hast no right to enforce, but here right is enforced against thee. Or, to put it in the words of viii. 1-3: "Not thou has known God, but God knows thee." That, as we saw in i. 1, he is an apostle by the will of God, and not by virtue of his religious talent; that he did not find God, but God found him and set him on his path, took him captive, entrusted him with his stewardship, without making any covenant with him, without making him promises for his person, simply as the Lord who can command, as a compelling necessity (ix. 16)—this fact now finds expression in the fact that while in possession of his freedom he is bound, while in possession of the fullest power he is obliged to *abstain*. It is, in fact, the freedom and power of the apostle—that is, the freedom and power bestowed upon him by God, and not his personal freedom and power. ix. 19-23 describes what this means for him: it means that as the holder of his office he must everywhere and always be just what he is *not* as a man. Why? Because he has to discharge his office towards other men. And, because they are other men, whether he likes it or not, they are always just what he himself is not. If he wanted to assert himself, he could not discharge his office. Constraint is upon him. God is in the scheme with *His* right. Upon this is shattered his human right to self-assertion, as thus: to become a servant, to become a Jew, to become a man under the law, perhaps even to become a man without the law, to become a weak man, to become all things—wherefore? In order to win, in order to save, in order to carry out the office committed to me, which is more important than my person and its justifiable claim upon life, in order not to lose my own share in the gospel (ix. 23), in order that, while I may be preaching to others, I may not wear myself out and become a castaway (ix. 27). The metaphor of the runner in the race (ix. 24-26) illus·trates what he means. A victorious contest is impossible without self-discipline! Consequently, because Paul is such a runner in the stadium, not by his own, but by God's will, not for a corruptible, but for an incorruptible crown, limits are set to his freedom, and hence he *will* not do everything he is undoubtedly permitted to do.

The tenth chapter is obviously connected with ix. 27, where Paul threatened himself: "What if I, although an apostle, and as an apostle, should come to grief?" This would happen, he opines, if, perchance, I should exercise any other freedom than the freedom of God which imposes limits to my freedom. If that be done, if you Christians of Corinth, with your human knowledge and the laxer practice that goes with it, perhaps do this, then you will become like the people of Israel in the wilderness (x. 1 *et seq.*) who, in spite of the most wondrous proofs of divine grace, found only the slightest portion of God's favour. What, then, was their case? They lusted after evil things; they ate and drank; they whored and tempted the Lord and prayed to idols, and, instead of favour upon favour, punishment upon punishment began to assail them. But *that* is not the meaning! Might not the meaning of freedom have been something like this: That in face of this purer, deeper insight that God alone is God, the idols in the world are again invested in their rights, quite harmlessly and in the joyful consciousness that they are not dangerous, that to the pure all things are pure, that all things are lawful? Might not this have been the meaning of, and the way in which we are to interpret, the wonderful Pauline doctrine of the sovereignty of God—of the unconstraint in which His children may and will serve Him in the midst of the world, of the free and self-confident flexibility of the Christian conscience? Might it not be possible to discover an excellent Pauline foundation for the despised service of the world and idolatry, and then, at any rate, to be "free" and call oneself a Christian, but as a "free" Christian to come to grief most ignominiously? Paul does not say that this is the case with the Corinthians, but he warns them: "All . . . were under the cloud, and all passed through the sea; and were baptized unto Moses in the cloud and in the sea," he says, with a happy allegorical touch, in x. 1-2, and we are reminded of viii. 1: "We *all* have knowledge." Christ, with His spiritual meat and drink, was in their midst, x. 2-4 states bluntly—but x. 5: With many of them God was not well pleased . . . and they were destroyed of the destroyer (x. 10). Therefore: "Let him that thinketh he stand take heed lest he fall" (x. 12). Obviously, what temptation is, the claim to dominion of a world hostile to God, offered, not to its own children, but to God's elect, with all the awfulness of backsliding and getting lost that lurks behind it, they do not yet know. God's faithfulness alone is a match for the force of this claim. It is above the secular power, and, when temptation comes, it provides a way of escape for its own, so that they are able to endure and conquer it (x. 13). It is just God! Therefore, flee idolatry! (x. 14). The word was uttered in x. 7. Paul does not spare his readers hearing it again. Only by virtue of God's faithfulness is it true that the pagan-sacramental sphere, which they enter when they buy and eat flesh that has been offered to idols, is not dangerous to them because it is profane. Merely by virtue of their *human* knowledge this is not true. What the Corinthians are thinking of, their consciousness of freedom and superiority, does not protect them from idolatry, from the reality of temptation, to which only the quite other reality of God is superior. Paul appeals to the reader's intelligence, to his discriminating capacity (x. 5). The Lord's Supper which Christians celebrate or, more strictly, the reality of God which is designated by the Lord's Supper, or, according to xi. 26, announced thereby, is living communion with Christ (x. 16), (and, as x. 17 shows, Paul immediately identifies this with their living communion with one another), just as the sacrifice in Israel designated, preached, and guaranteed "the communion of the altar" (what is meant is the community of those sacrificing upon the altar) with God. What, however, is the communion into which they enter who sacrifice to idols, or even only sojourn in the whole sphere of this sacrifice, in the incense of the pagan world of religion? Certainly, meat offered to idols is nothing in itself, and the place whither it is brought is also nothing in itself. In uttering this warning it did not perhaps occur to Paul to take the pagan world of religion seriously as a magical element in nature (x. 19), but that sacrifices are here offered to devils and not to God—that, at any rate, is something. It goes without saying that Paul was familiar with contemporary ideas and customs, especially those relating to sacramental eating and drinking: as, for example, the wholly secular banquets which were expressly and solemnly arranged under the auspices of Serapis, Anubis, Jupiter, and Hercules (details of which are quoted in Lietzmann's commentary on these verses). But I do not believe that this contemporary historical interpretation can supply the clue in the understanding of the passage. Paul was quite serious, whatever he may have thought *in concreto* (and he was, of course, thinking of perfectly concrete things), when in viii. 5 he said: Not idols as such and idols' meat as such, but gods and lords exist. The devils are the invisible, but extremely real, world powers, from whence came the temptation to which the majority of the Israelites succumbed in the wilderness, and the strength of which even exceeds the strength of Christians. These world powers constitute the meaning, the object, and the reality of pagan idolatry. Whatever its gods are called, paganism is the worship of devils, the religious veneration of world spirits and world forces instead of God. To be in contact with this atmosphere and not to be severed from paganism, that which the Corinthians cherish and prize as their freedom, may, regarded objectively, be communion with devils *every time,* and the subjective element, their human knowledge, will not prevent its actually being so. Then the comrade of Christ becomes the comrade of devils; blind just because of his knowledge, upon which he builds, he falls into their hands. Subjectively one may be an absolutely honest Christian, full of the most sincere confidence in his pure conscience and in the "all things are lawful for me," and objectively may serve the devil as long as he lives, and will and may not once observe it just because of his certitude! And then arises the Either-Or which Paul sketches in x. 20-21. Ye cannot drink the cup of the Lord and the cup of devils; ye cannot be partaker of the Lord's table and of the table of devils. Ye *cannot.* If you do so—and what guarantees you against doing so? your freedom perhaps!—then the cup and the table of the Lord become nothing but lies, nothing but Greek religious magic, like others may also have. In the formula "Christianity and   . . ." lurks betrayal of Christianity, backsliding and perishing. In the face of this threatening danger, it is not the free disposition of man that is the abode of the real, the sacred freedom, but the freedom alone that God has and confers. We are not to challenge God, to provoke Him to anger by presumption, by aiming to be stronger than He, by recklessly availing ourselves of our freedom, where He in His freedom perhaps just halts, and also bids us halt (x. 22). That is what

Paul designs to offer as food for reflection to the discriminating faculties of the Corinthians, and, indeed, of his own supporters in Corinth in particular. Is not your freedom perchance this freedom from the fear and the trembling of the man of God, who has to be faithful not so much to himself as to his Lord? If it were that, then would judgment already be upon you. If it be not that, then it cannot profess to be an unrestricted freedom.

"All things are not expedient; all things edify not," we now read again in x. 23, as in vi. 12, but on a higher plane and in a dialectically more refined connexion than there. But what is the limitation planted in freedom by God? I would not say, like Lietzmann, that x. 17, with its at first surprising emphasis upon *communio*—the idea of the Lord's Supper applied to the Church—is a digression from the main thought. Rather the plain steering direct to the leading thought is the explanation of the verse. The communion with Christ is in Paul's view not to be severed from the communion in the Church. In x. 24 occurs the same injunction that is placed right at the beginning of the similar section Rom. xiv.-xv. Let no man seek his own, but every man another's. Paul has already said what is vital upon this in viii. 8-13. His concern for the Corinthian gnostics and what they understood by freedom then prompted him to make this further digression ix. 1-10. We must now go back to those verses in the eighth chapter. Making use of that freedom has in itself no positive value. To eat questionable meat does not commend us to God; to refrain from eating signifies no deprivation; to eat is no gain (viii. 8). But there is more than one "weak one" in the Church, who has not the right knowledge, the freedom and superiority which spring from the right conception of the idea of God. He makes the eating of that meat a matter of conscience. A regrettable restriction, certainly. As we saw, Paul does not conceal what he thinks of the matter. But how unimportant is this deficiency compared with the fact that he is a brother for whom Christ died (viii. 13). The use that the Pauline gnostic makes of his freedom may become a stumbling-block to him, may cause him to follow his example without the approbation of his conscience (viii. 9-10), and through that he will perish (viii. 11). What Paul thought about conscience was this: our own good conscience gives us no charter, does not preserve us from temptation, which only God can do. But in the alien good conscience, in the personality of another, as it is constituted, with its possibilities and limitations, we meet the inviolable majesty itself, the insurmountable check set upon our liberty. The Church may not be torn asunder. We know why: its communion is identical with the communion of the body and blood of the Lord (x. 16, 17). Hence, he who sins against his brother by such maltreatment of another's conscience sins against *Christ* (viii. 12). And hence, Paul continues (viii. 13) impetuously: If my eating is an offence to my brother, I will eat no flesh to all eternity. Mention has already been made of the pastoral advice which Paul gives upon the basis of this whole reflection (x. 25-30). The conclusion of the section. (x. 31-33) shows that the question of sacrificing to idols, and its answer, was really only the occasion, but not the theme. Whether ye eat or drink, do all to the glory of God. With the vexatious modern idea that the whole of life, including eating and drinking, must be, and can be, a service of God, this, of course, has nothing to do. Paul is not concerned with eating and drinking and the other activities of man, but with using or not using the freedom that is founded in the knowledge of God. What is done in the freedom of God, really in the freedom derived from God, in the knowledge that is no puffing up of man but is his being known of God (viii. 3), that is done to the *honour* of *God*. In this sense, the Corinthians are enjoined to aim at giving no offence (x. 32); what is meant is that they are not, through excessive religious confidence, to be the cause of stumbling-blocks, but to be bearers of the *testimony* of God, and for God's honour. But it is remarkable that Paul only says the first, the negative: not to be in the way of God through our inflated pride is what we can do for God's honour. The sweep is immeasurably wide in these two last verses: Paul visualises his Corinthians who are just nearest to him and who have understood him so well and yet have not understood him at all, provided they will take to heart his sharp warning, standing before Jews and Greeks and the Church of God, responsible and capable of responsibility, because they know that they are not to be concerned with seeking their own profit, that which is good for oneself, be it ever so good or so spiritual or so well founded, but that of the many, and that is: their *salvation*. For Paul it is the same as if he had once more said: *God's* cause. In this sense he wants to regard the Corinthians as his

successors (xi. 1). Like the angel of the Lord upon
the path of Balaam, the great riddle once more looms
across a human path, or even a solution of all riddles.
Truly, it was no bad way that these Pauline gnostics
took; an abundance of truth and strength was there,
but Paul's petition points the Corinthians to the
better, as well as to the *worse,* way. Both the one
and the other must accept the meeting with *God* at
first as the end *of their* path.

§ 6

The next of the four chapters which still separate
us from our goal, chapter xi., stands by itself. It is
a remarkable chapter not only in its first part, but
also in the second. Reference is made to two details
of Christian Church life, respecting which Paul has
to give advice or lay down rules. xi. 2-16 deals with
the *veiling* of *women* in the Church meeting. The
passage is perhaps one of the most difficult in Paul's
writings. Conditions of the most concrete kind,
grounded upon contemporary culture and civiliza-
tion, and again what are plainly incidental and individual opinions of Paul of the most concrete kind,
seem to have got into an inextricable entanglement
so far as we are concerned. A question, for the
significance of which we at first lack all comprehension, is treated with a fullness of detail which is
almost a matter for astonishment and according to a
method which, for us, is quite unconvincing. We
need not be surprised that a modern exegete, rejoicing in the considerable contemporary data which he
assembles here in a way deserving of our gratitude,

eventually groans: "The guiding ideas of the following demonstration are totally incomprehensible to
us." I do not, however, feel disposed to surrender
forthwith. When we look at the matter, it is only
the *substance* that is totally impenetrable: in xi.
2-10, the meaning of the *custom* of veiling woman,
and man going bareheaded, and in verses 13-15, the
alleged *natural order* that man must wear short and
woman long hair, a principle to which Calvin deli-
cately objected in a sermon upon this text, referring
to the old Gauls and Teutons (*Op.* xlix. 743). But
let us take this matter as we find it, i.e. as a custom
which was the definite rule then and there, and which
Paul, for reasons which cannot further be established, considered to be right in itself. With such a
man as Paul, the substance need not be taken so
tragically, whether the intention be to elucidate its
pragmatical aspect, or whether this is, as here, not
the case. The assumption of the passage is that
there was a disposition in Corinth to *abolish* the
custom. This must, then, have been the expression
of a tendency to make the superiority of man over
woman invisible, or even to deny it altogether.
Fashions are the expression of outlooks on life. In
deprecating the fashion, Paul deprecates the outlook
on life which it embodies. Paul's own tenets are to
be understood as the expression of an opposite outlook on life. Whoever is otherwise acquainted with
Paul will not be surprised to learn that what we meet
with here is also a conservative outlook on life. He
is not the man to support a more or less powerful
tendency designed to effect a transformation in the
customary relation of the sexes. He represents the

patriarchal principle that woman should be subordinate to man.   It is open to argument whether this opinion is calculated to render the obscurity, that is, what is to be understood only contingently, less obscure, or whether what we are concerned with here is an insight springing from ripe wisdom into the natural limitation of human life, the significance of which goes beyond an arguable opinion.   Paul expressly declares his concrete judgment upon the *covering* (of women) to be arguable; verse 16 teaches this, and, in point of meaning, should be compared with verses 7, 12.   ("But to the rest, speak I, not the Lord.")   Whether Paul also said that from the *outlook on life* at the back of this judgment, is another question, probably *not*.   But this question is not decisive.   In my opinion, Paul can be understood in the main—what he *means* he *says,* although one cannot endorse the attitude towards man and woman which emerges here, as in chapter vii. with his opinion of marriage, or here, with his pronouncement upon the fashion in question.   Obviously, behind his outlook on life here disclosed, there is still something else, a *third* something: a principle which neither stands nor falls with this outlook on life, but which *finds expression* for him in this outlook on life; and that is the principle that it is better, more obvious, more intelligent, in life's relations of subordination that are naturally given, to revere the majesty of God than, out of liberal indifference or because protesting is enjoyable, to scorn this primitive, not unequivocal, not eternal, but at any rate perceptible, word of God.   This passage, too, although in another sense, is a parallel to Rom. xiii.

Let us, then, assume as given: Paul affirms *in concreto* the subordination of woman to man to be a case to which that principle is to be applied, and we learn how he, prompted by that *concretissimum,* the veiling question, effects the application: xi. 3, the metaphor of a four-runged ladder downwards: God, Christ, Man, Woman, always the higher of the lower "head." "*Kephāle,*" means, in addition to head, also sum, connexion, origin, and end. It is clear that in the relation of Christ to man, that has a totally different application from the relation of man to woman. But it *applies,* Paul means, as much or as little as anything can apply in the corruptible shape of life and order of life amidst which we find ourselves. It is important that even in the relation between man and woman there are plain and insurmountable barriers (insurmountable at least within this world). These barriers point us to above. By their incomprehensible and yet so palpable existence, they remind us of that altogether other incomprehensible existence, of the Head of the Church in heaven, whose Head is God Himself, of the origin and end *par excellence,* of the first origin and the last end. In this sense, woman is to consent to her subordination to man, but man, too, shall observe this subordination, not for the sake of his own dignity, but for the sake of the dignity of the order whose representative he is on earth. The man who covers his head in the community—that is, masquerades as a woman—dishonours his Head, Christ (xi. 4). He forgets, not his manly honour, but the finger-post to above, which is the real meaning of his manhood. And every woman who is uncovered in the Church dishonours her head, the man, not by her rebellion against him as man, which is expressed in negligent manner, but by her rebellion against the order, which she encounters in him, by her forgetting what man signifies for her (xi. 5). She must have carried the neglect of manners, perhaps, somewhat further still (let her also be shorn), in order to demonstrate to herself and everybody *ad oculos* upon what *path* she was treading. If she will not do this, then let her refrain from that (xi. 6). xi. 7-10 is a variation of the fundamental idea of xi. 3: A man is to assert his manhood as the created image of God, as God's reflection upon earth, first created, not for the sake of woman. And hence woman must wear on her head in the Church a sign of the power that is established over her, not the power of man as such, but the power of God over His creatures represented by man. The power, authority, is in fact the covering. The last words of xi. 10, "because of the angels," are difficult—what are they doing here? It was Tertullian—who was probably somewhat obsessed with such things—who first gave currency to the explanation that the angels in question were the fallen angels mentioned in Gen. vi. 1 *et seq.*, with their lust after the daughters of men, because they were fair, and Lietzmann thinks that the numerous contemporary parallels to this idea constrain us to accept this explanation, although he perceives, and himself confesses, that they "are completely foreign to the context." The phrase "because of the angels" only fits into the context because it forms a repetition of the "For this cause" at the beginning of the verse. In that case, however, the explanation must be sought in Calvin's direction: If women begin to masquerade as men in the Church, they thereby manifest their dishonour to the angels of Christ (the angels who serve praying believers); they make them into witnesses of the dissolution of the order of which they are guilty! And that is to be avoided! Apart from what has been said above, the explanation of the notion of the unconditional superiority of man revealed by xi. 1-10 is to be sought in xi. 11-12, where we are at once reminded that the same Paul (Gal. iii. 28) also knows that in Christ there is neither male nor female. In the Lord, is neither the man without the woman, *nor vice versa;* but all things from God. The question is not one of different relation to God; compared with the great distance between God and man the little distance between woman and man is not without importance, not at all, but it is still really small, quite small, in fact nugatory. Nor is the question one of temporal order, as such, but of the divine order manifested in it—and that is twofold. In the time of Paul, Christianity was still too good to surrender itself to the sanctification of such an earthly order. Women are not to let this perturb them, said Calvin in the Geneva Chancellery: The main thing they have and enjoy! "It is a little thing that in this world we have some little superiority: for the whole is only a metaphor. A corruptible splendour!" (*Op.* xlix. 728). This is undoubtedly Paul's opinion. But we are dealing with an *order,* that is what he means here. xi. 13-15 will then, with more or less success and penetration, attempt to show how this order is also akin to nature, and xi. 16 closes with the statement:

in the "Churches of God" this order has so far been valid, and this ought to be known in Corinth.   If we have so far rightly interpreted the whole spirit of the Epistle, we may also be permitted to place in the series this piece, this halt, which sounds this time in a very unexpected place and yet proceeds from a direction that is now no longer unknown to us, according to its critical tendency, "from God."

And likewise, it now also asserts with the second half of the chapter.   In xi. 17-33, too, we are dealing with a repudiation of a powerfully flourishing type of man in the Corinthian Church, with his tendency to wilful and self-seeking assertion of his influence. It is that which connects the two halves of the chapter.   Here, as there, it is, for the rest, in phenomena peculiar to religious life in Corinth that Paul sees this tendency in operation;   there, in the breaking down of the barrier between man and woman, here, in the *divisions,* which, already mentioned and discussed in the first chapter, seem to have broken out directly in divine service, and then, above all, in the profanation, in fact the dissipation, of the *sacrament of the Lord's Supper.*   Glancing at both, Paul says (xi. 17):   Your coming together, your cultus, serves the worse rather than the better, and is become a direct danger.   Into the first point, verses 17-19, Paul does not enter more closely.   He foresees that from the divisions and the formation of groups, whatever their aim might be, spring the dissensions, "schisms," which necessarily arise from party opinions emphasized with individual presumption, and he pronounces this judgment upon the Church!   For this is the meaning of xi. 19.   The δόχιμοι, in this case:

those who do not take part in these divisions will
then be made manifest; the rest need not be said.
The question of the *Lord's Supper* comes up for
discussion incidentally. Here also, a type of egoism
of a simple and probably not of a merely material-
istic character, but of a spiritual and intellectual
nature, has spread. This meal, which has its meaning and place in the Christian Church only in the
paradoxical form of an unconditional communion of
all, high and low, has in Corinth developed into
something apparently more refined—that is to say, a
kind of festal banquet of the prosperous and probably also the educated among themselves, at which
the poor must look on from a distance (xi. 21). Just
because of this it is a profanation to make of the
Lord's Supper a *Supper of Men* (xi. 20-21), similar
to the pagan religious feasts, an affair which the
participants, as Paul sarcastically opines, could also
settle at home (xi. 22*a*). It is despising the Church
of God and shaming those that have not, he bursts
out angrily in xi. 22*b*, with the whole weight of his
authority, placing himself protectively in front of the
latter and in sharp antagonism to the prosperous.
But then he turns over the leaf: an attack on the
meal of the communion is an attack on the institu-
tion of the Lord Jesus, which he, Paul, delivered to
the pure Church as he received it from the Lord (xi.
23). Note how the expressions "received" and "delivered" occur here, which we shall again encounter
in reversed order in xv. 3. The meaning in both
cases is: With what has now to be said, we are dealing, not with Pauline theology, nor with information
from historical sources of oral or written nature,

and thus not with matters about which this or that opinion might be held in the Church of Christ, but as regards the speaker, with the word of Kyrios, the Lord Himself, and consequently for the listener with the severing alternative: for or against the Lord: "I have received it from the Lord. The Lord Himself repeated to him, Paul, what He said as the Founder of the Supper": "in the night, when the Lord Jesus was betrayed. . . ." By this categorical assertion, Paul does not mean to guarantee, which would interest us, that these were the authentic words of the so-called historical Jesus. For what we call the historical Jesus, a Jesus pure and simple, who is not the Lord Jesus, but an earthly phenomenon among others to be objectively discovered, detached from His *Lordship* in the Church of God, apart from the *revelation* given in the Jesus of the Church and at first to the apostles—this abstraction was for Paul (and not for him alone) an impossible idea. The thought that Jesus should and could be first regarded by himself, in order then to recognize Him as Lord, could at most be for him a painful recollection of his former error. *This* Jesus, who is not the *Lord*, who is known *after the flesh* (2 Cor. v. 16), was in fact the foe whom he persecuted; he no longer knows Him. But Paul is not now reflecting on what this Jesus, who was known after the flesh, might have said on the occasion of the Supper, but upon what *Kyrios* Jesus, the Lord of the *Church*, said to him, Paul, when He made him His ambassador. The Lord does not live for him in the oldest, best-attested or most credible tradition—why should it be just the Lord who lives and speaks there?—but in His supreme present *revelation* to His *Church, in concreto,* in the herald's commission which it has become to Paul. He reported *direct* from the source: The Lord *Himself* is the tradition. That each of the individual words in which he discharges this commission has its human earthly genesis, history, and limitation, that these words of the Lord in his mouth, received from the Lord Himself, are in his pen influenced by the currents of contemporary trends of thought, he himself would probably have at least disputed. But this again, positively and negatively, had and has the least to do with *the* genesis, history, and limitation, by virtue of which he, as a man living in the Hellenic age, was an *apostle* of *Jesus Christ.* Paul, therefore, does not *prove,* but he *testifies* what the will of the Founder is concerning this Supper, as it is actually celebrated in the Church. Almost at the first glance, the things he was chiefly concerned with may be perceived: (xi. 24-25) "this do in remembrance of Me!" Bread and wine, not in itself but eaten and drunk (where just *this* bread and the cup (xi. 26) are enjoyed in the *Church*), are the visible equivalents of the body and blood of the Lord, *"for you,"* as the New Testament (xi. 24-25). Wherefore these equivalents? "In remembrance; (xi. 26) ye proclaim thereby the death of the Lord until He comes." Paul's interest is not, as in a later age, fixed on the relation of element and thing, but on the action as such. Those who take part in it thereby proclaim (upon that which they *receive* Paul lays no stress) that they know their Lord, that, although outwardly invisible, He is immediately present with them like that which

they eat and drink. In fact, they eat the bread and
drink the cup of the *Lord* (xi. 27), and, indeed, of
the crucified Lord, who will come again bringing
with Him the end of all things, even the end of all
such celebrations. Obviously what Paul means is
that, during this celebration, the shadow which
Christ casts over the whole of life on this side of the
grave cannot be forgotten. Can this action be performed in the Church without shuddering at the
great preliminariness with which this, our world, "in
the night when the Lord Jesus was betrayed," was
characterized for ever? without fear and trembling
before the narrow door which leads to life? Can
this Supper ever be anything else than what it was
at first, a *farewell supper,* at which the anxious look
of man can only come to rest in the light beyond the
grave? Is not hope, the hope of life, which is still
inseparably bound up with the remembrance of the
Lord who died for us, impossible where the severity
of this death is forgotten? And it is just that, this
forgetting just where they ought to be *remembering,*
this unworthy eating and drinking, which is not dedi-
cated in a serious religious spirit to the critical
severity of the matter, and which is even altogether
profane, with which Paul now reproaches the Corinthians. That this is so is decisively shown for him
by the manner, described in xi. 20 *et seq.,* in which
they have destroyed the *communio* of the alleged
feast of love. "They are guilty of the body and
blood of the Lord" (xi. 27). They reel drunkenly
(and that not only figuratively xi. 21) along the road
which the other religious fellowships boldly tread,
but which shall be *closed* to *them* with iron bolts, if

they intend to dishonour the gift given in the death
of Christ.   The Lord's Supper is a question that is
addressed to man xi. 28.   Cross and finality speak to
him there; he should ask himself whether he fares
well or ill with his hope of a future life, and *then*
eat and drink.   Otherwise (xi. 20, the threatening
tone of xi. 19 returns), by not subjecting himself to
this interrogation he incurs the condemnation, which
he would have overcome in veritable remembrance
of the Lord.   He eats and drinks in his alleged Christian, but in reality paganly profane religious feast,
that which must befall the *world*, the doom.   Paul
can already see this judgment operating in their
midst (xi. 30-32): weakness, disease, death are not
incidents that go without saying, not so easily understood as by later Christian ages as ordinances of
God, which are to be accepted with resignation; no,
gloomy proofs that even Christians are still firmly
rooted in the *world*, that redemption is still distant
even for them, that even over them God's chastising
hand is still outstretched.   If we address ourselves,
as we ought, to the question put to us by the Lord,
and therefore enter into living hope in Him, we shall
escape the judgment.   May it, at least, serve us as
a warning, so that we shall not incur damnation in
the last judgment.   How drastic is the criticism
persistently applied in the First Epistle to the
Corinthian Church, not only in fact on account of
the special external conditions in Corinth, but obviously even more on account of the decisive criterion
which Paul applies, is plainly shown by the second
half of the eleventh chapter, in which he fearlessly
declares to his readers that the centre of their

Church life, their divine service, is a danger. Paul
regarded the possibility that the Church might become empty under this threat as less evil than the
other, that it might remain full of rank weeds of
humanity.

§ 7

Chapters xii.-xiv., which now remain to be discussed, again form a consistent whole. It is only
here that we gain complete insight into the almost
dazzling wealth of spiritual and religious life, despite,
and besides, everything pointing in an apparently
opposite direction, in which this Church must have
abounded, and of which Paul speaks in i. 4 *et seq.*
allusively and certainly not in a spirit of exagger-
ation. In no case may we conceive the Corinthian
Church merely as a den of partisan squabblers, un-
controlled sexuality, stubborn ascetics, and luxu-
riant gourmandizing. Certainly all these things
existed in crude, unadorned vitality, and also no
doubt in refined and religious disguise. But by their
side, see chapters xii. and xiv., what an abundance
of high, even the highest, potentialities, which were
indeed taken very seriously by Paul as spiritual
charism! It is, in fact, a superabundance of spirits,
forces, and gifts which prompts Paul to utter his
urgent exhortation to *unity* in chapter xii. and to
observe the right *order* and subordination in chapter
xiv. The last and strongest powers, even of the good
and divine (at least, Paul so regarded it), so far as
we can speak of the powers of the good and of the
divine in man, together with all kinds of dæmons
of the great pagan city, which are even doing their

mischievous work in the Church of God, appear to be let loose here, and this other task which devolves on Paul, of mastering this explosion of the Spirit and of spirits, to assert and enforce a still higher standpoint even against all these extreme possibilities, seems to be an even more difficult task than warding off evil. If we think of the society described by Dostoievski we shall be able to gain some understanding of the picture. With the picture they unroll, chapters xii.-xiv. have something of the end of history about them, or, perhaps we should say, something bordering on the end of history. Thus it came about that such springs as are almost only to be regarded with head-shakings burst forth, when into a spiritually agitated and already religiously excited population the idea of the last things was hurled with a penetrating severity, which was subsequently imitated but never achieved such an effect. However the incidents described may be judged, we feel at any rate that here we are hovering at the frontiers of humanity.

What is still conceivable beyond all these voices that are here audible? The troubled sea of spiritualistic and theosophical illuminations and gifts? Are we not already partly in the midst of it? The bliss and terrors of hysterical hallucination and intuition which should be more the concern of the nerve specialist than of us theologians? Have we not already crossed even this boundary? Or suicide, like that of the philosopher who plunged into the crater of Etna in order to solve the world riddle, a really most obvious idea, when the stages of prophecy and *gnosis* have, as here, been reached and

overstepped? Or perhaps the saving step backward
into the orderly limits of a healthy bourgeois religious moderation? But if it is *not* any of these
things, what is it then? More urgently than anywhere in our Epistle we find in chapters xii. and xiv.
the need of a word of redemption, just in the midst
of this human world so full of the Spirit and so full
of God, and for that appearing so unredeemed.
And, in fact, immediately afterwards the decisive
word of the resurrection falls. As is, however, well
known, a decisive word which fundamentally outbids
the whole surroundings is already uttered in the
midst of this section itself, in the great intermediate
fragment of chapter xiii. We should not rush at the
explanation of 1 Cor. xiii. The word "love" is soon
pronounced, but what is "love"? when the higher
and most perfect possibilities, if not absolutely the
first among the best, have manifested themselves all
round, including some which truly seem to represent
what is usually called "love"! What is indicated
in chapter xiii. is a great passing away of all those
things that are not love, once more death: the
highest and best gifts in seriousness, an utter depre-
ciation of all the things that are to be found on this
side of that boundary of humanity. Love *alone*
never ceases; only *it* is, in xiii. 12, placed in relation
to the seeing of God face to face which will take
place in the beyond of all time, in the eschatological
"then." If Paul is now in earnest, in chapter xii.
and xiv., with that positive appraisement of the other
gifts of the Spirit, and, on the other hand, is in
earnest with this quite isolated and attention-com-
pelling declaration upon love, then what we have

to do with in chapter xiii. is a direct prelude to the
theme of which chapter xv. will treat. Or, in other
words, in chapter xiii. we already find ourselves in
the midst of eschatology, only here regarded from
the standpoint of man, for it is out of the question
that, as appears more or less distinctly in many
interpretations, Paul calculated, by using the word
"love," to point the way backwards out of the world
of Spirit and of spirits into the world of the intelligible, the healthy, and the normal. His description
of love really does not warrant that interpretation.
This chapter rather shows, obviously in the sense of
the construction we have hitherto placed upon the
rest of the Epistle regarding the activities of man
as such, and now, therefore, without any ambiguity:
even the gifted and the inspired, even spiritual man
as such beyond the point where there is an end of
him as man, where it says of the best gifts that they
are "in part" and that "they will pass," where the
highest peaks of earthly mountains remain under
our feet, where man, from the human standpoint,
would in fact live in the free air, were he not just
there sustained by God, were not salvation and redemption there from the altogether other side, where
—the idea of viii. 2 here recurs—the knowledge of
God and the being-known by Him (xiii. 12) coincide
in one. In chapter xiii. a human possibility is shown
as the last of all among the last things: thus it must
be connected with chapters xii.-xiv.; but, in truth, if
xiii. 1-8 be read intelligently, it cannot fail to be
apparent that *this* human possibility is just *God's*
possibility for man. Like lightning in the midst of
clouds is the effect of chapter xiii., with its direct

reference to "a more excellent way" (xii. 31). The discussion of spiritual gifts, in fact, subsequently proceeds through a whole chapter. But the secret theme of the Epistle, the point at which all problems come and go, emerges for the first time in an independent trend of thought to which chapter xv. will revert with a new statement and conclusion.

Let us now make a rapid survey of the contents of the three chapters. Paul knows, as he says in xii. 1-13, that the entire sphere of the "pneumatics" —of the religious, as it would probably be best to translate the word—is an ambiguous sphere. Where does the dæmoniac start? Where does the divinely operative cease? Life, motion in itself, is no certain characteristic of the latter! Even the "dumb gods" know how to move their people. The name *Jesus* is for Paul the criterion before which the spirits separate. He who can curse Jesus surely does not speak in the Spirit of God, whereas the name Jesus Kyrios is impossible without this Spirit. No doubt it goes without saying that in both cases Paul was not merely thinking of the words Anathema and Kyrios, but of the whole attitude of the people in question, who are characterized by this or the other catch-phrase. But it is not of this criterion that he means to speak, but of the necessary unity of the agitation that is so dæmoniacally prominent in the Church, so far as there was occasion, according to xii. 1-3, to take it *seriously*, which was obviously *the case* to an extensive degree. We are able to form, to some extent, a concrete picture merely from the little that was said about such agitation.

Mention is made of Charisms and of administrations and of operations, and then of the word of wisdom, to be distinguished from the word of knowledge; then of faith, then of the gifts of healing, again to be distinguished from the working of miracles, from prophecy, of the gift of discerning spirits, which is obviously to be understood, according to the opening verses xii. 1-3, as speaking with tongues, and the art of such speaking. Later, in xii. 28-29, are added helps, governments, the gift of teaching. It is a whole, articulated, and mutually dependent cosmos. In the case of a number of these gifts we can safely assume that we are dealing with talents and capacities which are not unknown to us even to-day, and partly with such as we should reckon specially among the religious but generally among the spiritual. In the case of others, to be sure, we are in the presence of things which are to be explained, or rather are not to be explained, only from the analogies of the natural history of the great religious movements of all times, and in the case of yet others we are perhaps dealing with phenomena which never occurred before nor have ever recurred since. We must, as said, mentally draw a line along the side of what, according to our own ideas, is completely absurd, because Paul recognizes all these possibilities. But what might seem to *us* absurd was perhaps not really so to Paul, and for good reasons. It would be well to adopt an attitude of reserve and record the fact with astonishment. Whatever attitude we may adopt towards the "pneumatic" persons and conditions, the existence of which is assumed in 1 Cor. xii.-xiv., it is certain that Paul saw them in direct connexion with *Revelation*. He knows, as

xii. 1-3 shows, that he was dealing with phenomena of an ambiguous character, but he did not for a moment doubt that all of them within the sphere of ambiguity, which made a test necessary from time to time, could be real effects, words and proofs of God. The Spirit, the Kyrios, God speaks, works, dispenses, disposes—all the remarkable, strange, and perhaps repellent things that went on there before the eyes of the impartial observer of the Church. Paul sees the variety of religion—not in itself, for he knows that all this in itself could not happen in the Spirit of God, but standing under a *positive* sign of the *Church* of *Christ*. What interests us so much to-day—namely, the fact that all this has its exact counterparts in paganism—proves nothing whatever against it. What we are really concerned with is not phenomena in themselves, but with their whence? and whither? to what do they point? to what do they testify? That, however, is not the same thing within or without. Did not Paul himself make free, extensive, and familiar use of Greek thoughts, ideas, and sentiments? Thus, in dealing with the Church, he also reckons with the possibility that what was being enacted within, however great might be its relationship to what was without, is something totally different, and stands under a sign diametrically opposed to what was without.

At any rate, he takes his stand upon the ground of this possibility when he addresses the Church upon the subject. But just because of this, and to that extent, he also adopts a critical attitude towards it. The religious plenitude which he encounters in Corinth does not in itself impress him in the least.

It must be measured and tested at its source.
Discriminating severity means the idea of the divine
origin of a phenomenon just where it is dared to
think this thought. In the Church of the Lord are
these things, which in themselves others might also
have—divine *gifts*. That, however, is not a crowd of
gifted, inspired, and illuminated persons, not a place
of ever so wondrous details, peculiarities, accidents,
but the body of Christ, whose individual members
do not move individually, and cannot signify anything of themselves generally. Just because religion
is here seen in its most alien forms in connexion with
revelation, just because here the gifted, the inspired,
and the enlightened, the individual and the individual as such, are comprehended as being founded
directly in God—just because of this, the greatest
emphasis is placed upon *the same* Spirit, *the same*
Lord, and *the same* God (xii. 5-6). Just because in
and behind and over every individual is the One who
founded the Church, and the whole of the Church is
the embodiment of this One. Indifference towards,
or rebellion against, the whole is indifference towards, and rebellion against, the One; and if they
venture to appeal to revelation as the ground and
origin of their special talent, it is precisely this appeal that judged them. It is that which is expounded
at length, by means of the metaphor of the body and
its members, in the middle part xii. 12-20. The
passages that are decisive for the meaning of the
chapter are verse 6: "It is the same God which
worketh in all"; verse 7: "But the manifestation
of the Spirit is given to every man to profit withal"
("to profit" really means to collect, to co-operate, to

serve); verse 11: "But all these worketh *that* one
and the selfsame Spirit, dividing to every man
severally as He [the Spirit] will"; verse 18: "But
now hath God set the members every one of them
in the body, as it hath pleased Him." It is therefore not in spite of his individuality, but precisely
in his individuality, that every man is to stumble
against the limits imposed upon him. It is precisely
the absolute origin of religion that calls religion as
a human experience, even if it is a question of the
highest and truest, back into relativity, not to its
injury, for relativity is just its positive content, its
relation to its absolute origin. It is not thou who
hast made thyself just as thou art, but it is God's
thought and work based on His free will. The
peculiarity of the human individual, whose divine
imagery might be continuously transformed into
divine resemblance, must continually become that
which it is—a mirror, a witness to the peculiarity of
God. In the individual just as he is, in that wherein
he is not this or that, but strictly this quite specific
person—in him the one God can and will reveal
Himself. But this comes to pass only in *Christ,* in
His *Church,* in the *communion* of individuals: *it*
tells the individual what he is and can always become: the place of divine revelation. His particularity, his individual isolation in itself, is just the
opposite, namely: the place of revelation of hopeless
finality, limitation, the casualness of all created existence and—a blasphemy when in itself it is clothed
with pretension to be divine. That is obviously
what Paul tilts against in this chapter. In the name
of Majesty, Paul designs to appeal against the pre-

sumption, which the deplorable isolation of the spiritual or religious talent or genius confuses with the dignity of solitude, which the individual, whatever his special gift may be, derives from God. It comes to him only if and in so far as he sacrifices his very isolation, the tragically guilty magnitude of his standing on his own feet, his "I am that I am," and realizes that he stands and falls with others. In the name of Majesty, Paul is appealing to the bond which is to be found in freedom and to the freedom which is found in bondage. No isolation, no hypertrophy of the individual member as such. No competition, no struggle for existence of the members among themselves. Not each can be *each*, because God has appointed each to be *His*, in the Church, in the unity of the whole. But this distribution of gifts by God, because it happens through God, again signifies no rigid distribution, complete for all time. That each ought to know, according to verse 27, that, taken by himself, as a fragment ("in part" in the words of chapter xiii.), he is a member of the body, does not mean, because the body is the body of Christ, that each is to be and remain solely what he actually is. In the *suum cuique*, to each *his own*, which is at first the burden of chapter xii, is in fact concealed, despite the preliminary applicable "Are all apostles?" etc., verses 29-30, the compelling truth of the second power: To each the *One!* Hence verse 31: "Covet earnestly the best gifts!" This imperative command does not contradict the pronouncements in verses 6, 7, 11, 18, because in Paul's view there could be no competition at all between divine operations and human endeavour. Once

God's supreme rule in all human phenomena is *recognized* as a matter of basic principle, these also can again be *known* in their relative *distinctions* of higher and lower, important and unimportant, and the gravity of human decision for one or other activities can also again be referred to freely. Yea, the recognition of God's supreme sovereignty will then inevitably operate in just such matters, not because a man fatalistically reconciles himself to his definitely set peculiarity, but because a man ponders upon the differences in peculiarities and strives after the *higher*.

That God may be sought alters in no wise the fact that, when He is found, He is the God who, at His free pleasure, gives to whom and what He will. And that He is this God alters in no wise the fact that He may be sought from stage to stage, from the lower to the higher, to the highest gifts. In xiv. 1 Paul reverts to this differentiated expression: "Follow after" ("Covet earnestly"). At first he breaks off abruptly: "And yet show I unto you a more excellent way," a way incomparable of its kind that leads more directly to the goal than all other ways, even than the just exhorted "covet earnestly" to which Paul subsequently reverts, a *via maxime vialis,* "a way that is best adapted to travelling" (Bengel). With "Follow after love" Paul afterwards summarizes (xiv. 1) what he has said of this way, of all ways, but that is obviously only a feeble echo, returning to what he intended to say at first (xii. 31).

What is described in between: xiii. 1-13, at first stands quite by itself: no gift, no virtue, no state, no capacity, no experience which one can "follow" after, as after another possibility offered by God. In verses 1-3 love is distinctly enough set above all other gifts, including the highest. Distinctly enough is it (verses 8-10) eulogized as the final One, compared with the fragment ("in part"), the individual, against whom Paul warned so urgently in chapter xii. What he contemplated in chapter xii. obviously no longer suffices him here. The most serious recognition that God is near to each one of us in *His* manner seems from this standpoint, although it is complemented by the "covet earnestly the best gifts" (xii. 31), to be charged with a tension which presses for a solution and fulfilment.

It is, however fundamentally and profoundly it may be realized, a knowledge of God which, compared with the *real knowledge* of God, is as the speaking, thinking, and pondering of a child to that of a man (verse 11): it is a knowing through the glass (it is not necessary here to recall the imperfect metal mirror of antiquity: Paul simply means not a direct but an indirect knowledge, a knowledge in a strange medium, for it reflects itself in man and as human knowledge, and human knowledge means broken, that is indirect, knowledge). A knowledge in an "enigma," in the paradox of verse 12 (and how paradoxical is what Paul has to say about the relationship of the one God to the individual we have doubtless felt!). A knowledge "in part," in a word, although and just because, according to xii. 27, this "in part," the individuality of man through his incorporation in the body of Christ, is intended to be understood from God's standpoint as the witness to the one God. It is at best a dialectical knowledge, the two halves of the truth, which we cannot unite, sharply perceptible as such, but allowing none to perceive directly the Whole, that which is meant by the two sides. There "abideth" (verse 13) *not* this One, this Intended, to which it points. "When that which is perfect is come," then the partial knowledge and the prophecy will be done away with (verses 9-10); they fade and flutter away in all weathers, like Pauline theology (Paul was speaking deliberately in the first person and certainly not merely oratorically) before the sunshine and winds of truth. No, the perfect (verse 10), the manly and not childish knowledge of God, the seeing face to face (verse 12), the knowledge that my being known of God is adequate and comes at last, at last to peace in Him—that is beyond all, even all Pauline gnosis and prophecy. Here all divine revelations, and the human possibilities created by them, were they ever so significant, do *not* suffice. Here, too, there is no "covet earnestly," nor yet any "follow after"; no promotion from stage to stage. "They shall fail and shall cease" (verse 8). Everything which man, even the man who is inspired and impelled by God, can devise here as means, way, and bridge is insufficient. And not, indeed, because the earthly, the human, is in itself so imperfect, but because the perfect comes: *Because* the *sun* rises all lights are extinguished. And yet Paul obviously means: Upon what depends the Church of Christ, as just reckoned, touching this last thing? Upon what are we waiting unless it be that the perfect come, that we, from being children, become men, "see face

to face, know as we are known"? What else can
all the gifts and inspirations in our midst, however
surely they come from God—what else can all the
strivings after higher gifts, however surely com-
manded by God Himself, accomplish, except to
heighten the tension between the Now and the End,
between the appearance and reality, between time
and eternity, between our knowledge and the truth
sharpened to the point where it becomes unbearable? What is the despair of the children of the
world measured against the despair of the serious,
gifted Christian impelled by the Spirit, of the Christian who has experienced his God in the highest that
God can ever give him as man, and who, just as
such, is now forced to realize that as such he is
separated by an unbridgeable chasm from the goal,
whither the way upon which he is set (not of his own
reason, but through God!) yet leads? That is the
real meaning of the situation of the so highly and
richly favoured Corinthian Church, to which Paul
here feels impelled to refer with abrupt suddenness,
interrupting and correcting himself. In truth, he
cannot have been referring to a harmless prolongation or even widening of this way, upon which they
obviously already find themselves; even here he
pointed to a *via maxime vialis*, "a road that was best
suited for travelling." No, it is rather the end of all
theology, the end of all Christianity, the end of all
Churches, that is announced here, or, perhaps, the
beginning of all these things, the origin of all gifts of
grace ,the majesty to which he points so urgently in
chapter xii.: it announces itself here in words,
emerges from the background into the foreground.

This majesty is called a *way;* in a human doing—and above all in *not* doing—it expresses, at any rate, its powerful presence, and it cannot have been by accident that Paul went on to say: *"Follow after love"* (xiv. 1).

But the way of all ways must be this: the *divine* possibility in all human possibilities; speaking with tongues, prophecy, knowledge, martyrdom (verse 3), which Paul in chapter xii. took so seriously, and which he took so seriously just because of this, its divine possibility.   Now it is itself called by its name.   What were all the ways of men, even if they led direct from God to God, if not this: the reality of "from God to God" were as real as all its meaning, as the divine Yea which is pronounced over them, but which must also continue to be heard—from eternity, and hence ever *new* in time; from God, and hence for men always the incomprehensible *miracle?* "From God to God" never and nowhere goes without saying, is never and nowhere given. All ways may be cart-tracks, wrong turnings, by-paths (verses 1 *et seq.*): to speak with the tongues of men and of angels—a sounding brass or a tinkling cymbal—if I have no love. To know prophecy and all secrets and all knowledge and faith besides, the faith that removes mountains—yet I am nothing if I have not love. To give all that I have to the poor, to give my body to be burned, like the heroes of the Maccabean era—it avails me nothing if I have not love. There is *no* occasion to make a great sentimentality of this chapter, because Paul has called love the majesty which he introduces here so suddenly into the midst of the wondrously constructed

heaven of the Christian Church. Once we lose sight
of the sentimental-moral misunderstanding of the
word "love," there is, apart from xv., no chapter
in the whole Epistle wherein Paul has expressed in
such radical terms, and with such incisive severity,
what he had to urge in a critical spirit against the
Corinthian Christians. Whoever is not convinced
by verses 8-13 that what is actually referred to here
are the *last* things is invited to ascertain for himself
whether it is not a fact that almost everywhere
where the word "love" occurs in verses 1-7, such
a word as seriousness or hope or expectation could
be inserted without straining the meaning and in
view of 8-13, and whether we are not already
apparently standing in the midst of chapter xv.
Paul actually hinted at this in verse 13, when he
suddenly names faith and hope, besides love, as the
things which abide, when all else passes away, with
the coming of the Perfect. But he added: *love* is
the greatest of these, and the word which dominates
the chapter, claiming to be the redeeming word, is,
in fact, the word "love." What does "love" mean?
An altogether voluntary and selfless devotion to another, in any case. The language hitherto used in
the Epistle does not, however, permit us to think
of this other immediately and exclusively in terms
of other *men*. Where "love" has previously been
mentioned in the First Epistle to the Corinthians—
ii. 9 and viii. 1-3—the reference has been expressly
to love to *God*. Of course, a glance at verses 4-6
forbids us to adhere with one-sided closeness to this
meaning here. But with equal energy verse 7 again
warns us, with its declarations that can only, or

almost only, refer to love to God, against falling into the usual opposite one-sidedness. Rather are we enjoined from the outset, and all through, to keep our eyes fixed upon both at the same time, in accordance with the inseparable connexion, even the unity of the relation of the individual to the Lord and to the Church, which we have often encountered since chapter viii., and particularly in the context of the section chapters xii.-xiv. Love is just, to summarize the double-sided in one word, the vital element of the Church of Christ, that which constitutes it as such: the surrender of the isolated person, by which he ceases to be such; or we might as well say at once: the death which he dies as such, the total annihilation which he experiences as such, and then: his resurrection, now no longer as an isolated person, but as One in the service of his Lord, or, what comes to the same thing: as One in the Whole, who also is the Whole in him, the One. What a unique, eschatological event this indicates we can best see from the fact that in verses 4-7 love is described in a series of sentences that have a mainly negative purport, a certain indication that the last things, which can only be described *via negativa,* are in the immediate vicinity. That is the way in all ways: love, the act which is *not* self-understood by the isolated individual, that is, the really concrete man, apart from what he is in Christ. He cannot have patience, but it can. He does not know what is good, but it does. He is zealous (about having his right), but *not* love. He vaunts himself, but love does *not.* He puffs himself up (as Paul said in viii. 2 of the Pauline gnostics), but love does *not.*

He believes himself permitted and compelled to break down the barriers of convention; love does *not*. He seeks his own; love does *not*. He lets himself be provoked; love does *not*. He takes account of evil; love does *not*. He can rejoice if wrong is done to another; love rejoices only when truth conquers. He collapses now here, now there; doubts a little here, loses a little courage there; cedes little or much here: love bears all things, believes wholly, hopes wholly, endures wholly. Let whoever believes that the "love" of 1 Cor. xiii. might mean psychologically a Christian virtue that outbids all others, consider how he explains himself with this fourfold "all things" in verse 7, without elaboration. Not to mention the concluding "Love never faileth" (verse 8), which is best rendered by the classical Lutheran translation of "love never ceases to be," but emphasizing the "never" and carefully noting how immediately afterwards the abyss of "it shall vanish away" opens, before which all psychologically explicable Christianity, prophecy, and speaking with tongues, hopelessly find the ground vanishing under their feet. What is not love vanishes, whatever fine name it wears. And even that which wears the finest names lives only in and of love, and not of itself. Love alone never ceases. Is it not clear that by love in this place an act of man is described, but such an act as bursts the limits of psychological power to grasp, in which man has passed out of himself and behaves like one who he, as man, is not at all? Is it not as if the predicates which are here piled up on love simply *lift up* man the subject and set him in the air, where he loses his breath? For

when and where would man, the subject whom we
know, be anything else than just that atomized unit,
that individual, who constantly does what love does
not do?   Does love appear anywhere and anyhow
than as the vital element of the Church of Christ—
that is, however, in Christ Himself, in the miracle
that man does not perform, but which is performed
on him by God?   But no: Paul really indicates man
as the performer of this work.   Remarkable indeed
is his restraint in *not* saying the *loving man* does not
do this and that, but love emerges as an independent
person and acts for men.   But not without men, is
undoubtedly his opinion, else he would not have
spoken of a way, and would not have subsequently,
glancing back at the miracle of God that appeared,
been able to say: "Follow after love!"   The unique
feature of this chapter is that Paul here really
ventures to make man the subject of predicates,
from which the inference immediately suggests itself: here there is another man, a new creature;
"the old is passed away, behold the new is come"
(2 Cor. v. 17)—man himself and no one else.   In
the midst of the so variously flourishing springtide
of Corinthian Christianity comes the gospel—how
else, in fact, can it be called other than the gospel
of the resurrection of the dead, which at first meant
nothing less than that all this human life is condemned irretrievably to pass away, but whose subject is now just positively and precisely man, with
his corruptible living and doing, the creation of God,
and who must be redeemed by the same God?   It
is the great "transformation" and "putting on" of
incorruption and immortality of 1 Cor. xv. 51 *et*

seq. that is here already announced so authoritatively in the incomprehensible way which makes all other ways at the same time impassable and only now passable. Moreover, we can read both things out of this chapter: the severest *threat of judgment,* the sharpest attack on Christianity and its alleged possession; because even in spite of all that God has done to it, it is only Christianity—and the most shining *promise* which is made to it, because it is the Church of the Lord, the risen one, the new Adam, and therefore the end and the beginning. One thing only cannot be read out of this chapter: viz. what lies between end and beginnings, the senseless further enjoyment of the divine gifts, as though no crisis, no judgment, no promise awaited the Christian enjoying them. *No,* this crisis is *waiting* for salvation or perdition, or both: but certainly for the establishment of the full *sovereignty* of God, as certain as this—that "love never ceaseth."

§ 8

After chapter xiii., 1 Cor. xiv. signifies once more a descent to the plane of the rest of the Epistle, which was left at xii. 31. After suddenly pointing to the incomparable way, Paul resumes his discussion of the various comparable ways. The momentous "Follow after love" is followed by the easier "and desire spiritual gifts," which returns to the realm of experimental things, and then, as an explanation of "the best" xii. 31: most of all prophetic speech. It is this gradation, or at least part of a gradation among spiritual gifts, which Paul intends to emphasize in 1 Cor. xiv. For Paul means one thing in particular: prophetic speech is greater and better than speaking with tongues, however important and valuable he regards the latter to be (verses 4-5). "Strive after prophetic speech and do not suppress speaking with tongues" (verse 39). But above this special injunction is the general warning: "Let all things be done decently and in order" (verse 40). We can sum up. The criterion by which Paul compares with each other the phenomena of Christian Church life and tests them, is the idea of mutual and common edification. For us the word is refined to the point of unintelligibility, because we are accustomed in this connexion to think only of the subjective, the religious and spiritual enrichment and furtherance of the individual believer. For Paul, the subjective is related to the objective. It is therefore a question of edifying the Church, to be sure, through the effect upon the individual. The Church, which means here a community assembled for divine service, is, however, not a society whose purpose can be transformed according to the will of the individual, but it is rather itself originally the purpose, which all individuals have to serve, although indeed, just because, behind what impels and inspires the individuals are not merely their human free wills, but the spiritual gifts conferred on them by God. Only in the Church are they, in fact, gifts conferred by *God*. What is from God must serve to edify the Church and must be valued in the light of this object. We believe, however, that in Paul's mind "Church" was indirectly identical with Christ Himself as His visible manifestation. Edification does not apply to the abstract "community" or "Church," but to the community which testifies to *Christ*. The evidential value of the various spiritual gifts for those who are within and without is referred to again and again. That the trumpet gives a certain sound (verse 8) is the criterion of edification, and this also very properly describes the essence of the Church. It is difficult for us to-day to understand how Paul was at all in a position to affix a positive sign to such a phenomenon as glossolalia, where we are only able to see psychopathology and nothing else. This makes it difficult for us to understand the energy with which Paul then repels this phenomenon: "but strive more zealously after prophecy" (verses 1-5): the prophet is greater than he that speaketh with tongues (verse 5). We can no longer see the sacrifice, as such, that is here offered, even by Paul himself. It did not come to him so easily as it comes to us, to put speaking with tongues into the background. With every critical word that he utters upon this subject we must bear in mind that he was not concerned with something that was diseased, marvellous or exalted, but with a great, important, and divine possibility, which he did not want in any circumstances, to misjudge or suppress. He says of himself: "I thank my God, I speak with tongues more than you all" (verse 18). And he says expressly that he would like them all to be able to do so (verse 5). He valued speaking with tongues as something that was done for God (verses 2, 28), but also as an act of prayer and thanksgiving, to pray, to sing, to give thanks (verses 14-17), through which the person concerned, at least, edifies himself (verses 4, 28), and, beyond this, as a divine paradox, which is offered to the believer, as a negative testimony, so to speak, just as the prophets of Israel had occasionally to give their people (verses 21-22). But it can also serve to "edify the Church," if an intelligent interpretation be forthcoming (verses 5, 13, 28). And then nevertheless: not away with it, but push it back into the second rank, into the background! Once more: our attitude towards these things renders it much too *easy* for us to understand Paul with respect to this decision, so that we are liable just to *mis*understand him. The question for Paul, and for the Church, was something important, venerable, and vital, which ought to be discouraged at this point. We must not, therefore, seek to explain it in the light of what happened in Wales in 1903 and in Cassel and Grossalmerode in 1907. Such direct analogies may perhaps illustrate speaking with tongues *in itself,* as it occurred also in the cult of Dionysus, but not what Paul saw therein in the *Church* of *Christ* and not the significance of his decision, which was then cast substantially *against* it. In order to measure the importance of the operation which Paul performs here, we must remember that one might say the same thing, *mutatis mutandis,* about missions, or religious juvenile instruction, or the social activity of the Church. But he performs it. It is sufficiently remarkable how the same Paul, who, in chapters i., viii., and xiii., gave veritable proofs of the fact that he perceived the relativity of all gnosis, once again puts the question (verses 7-9), "How shall it be known?" quite in the middle; verses 14-19, plays human reason against the divine Spirit,

verses 23-33, so arranging all things that whatever
serves to edify the Church must be *understood*. He
sees therein that prophetic speech is to be preferred
to glossolalia: not as if it were there a question of
"inspired" speech, perhaps hard to understand, or
at any rate concealing a hidden thing (verse 25),
but speech which fundamentally proceeds from being understood, from knowledge. The folly of
preaching the Cross, the singularity of the Spirit of
God does *not* now just coincide with "becoming
children in understanding" (verse 20), with a cult
of the irrational. The divine wisdom does not consist in the fact that one does not know what is said
(verses 10, 16), in the paradox in itself, in the
absurdum of the *credo* as such. Paul was indeed not
sufficient of a pedant and schoolmaster to wish to
exclude the possibility of this absurdity; on the
contrary he confirms, in fact he demands it—as we
saw. The irrational has its place, but it is a subordinate place, and is not to be more than a way, a
point of transit. We are not to persist in it, not to
grow congealed in it, as if it were now *that*. Otherwise the ludicrous, the all too human is there, which
can appear in an irrational as well as a rational
shape. Passages like verses 7 *et seq.*, verses 16 *et
seq.*, verse 33, show that Paul was quite alive to the
humour of the thing. Inspiration in itself, which
does not lead to speaking, to relationship with the
non-inspired, to the imparting of knowledge, is nothing; let him keep silence in the Church, verse 28, is
the friendliest reference that is to be noted. As
surely as *gnosis* alone does not edify, so surely and
still less does glossolalia alone. If the gnostics and

the prophets must remember love, the speaker in an unknown tongue must remember gnosis and prophecy and reason, who knows what he says and who speaks to men and not to God or to himself (verses 2, 28). There is no human gift, even if it come from God, which is not destined to stumble against its limitations, which must not subordinate itself even were it to another contiguous human gift. The direct infinite subordination of man to God, which here also is the meaning of the whole, would, in fact, be illusion, if it were not really palpable through such subordination even in the finite. What the speaker with tongues, just he, must heed (with the gnostic a word is to speak for itself) is: "better five words with the understanding for the instruction of others than thousands of words in tongues" (verse 19); "Be perfect in understanding" (verse 20), and more words to the same effect that an inspired person would find hard to endure. Only when he can say this, is his inspiration genuine and legitimate. It is not reason in itself that is to be glorified and absolved by the placing of prophets and gnostics above speakers with tongues. Reason has its own limits. The limit of inspiration is just that which reason has by way of advantage over it, the discipline which man imposes upon himself if he wants to speak with understanding. "And the spirits of the prophets are subject to the prophets" (verse 32). This "subject" is wanting for the speakers with tongues. God, however, is not a God of confusion, but of peace (verse 33). From this standpoint they must perceive the relativity of their special gift. Incidentally inserted as this appears, verses 34-36, the famous passage: *"mulier taceat in ecclesia!"* "Let woman be silent in the assembly!" The idea of subordination emphasized in the preceding chapter, perhaps, too, the fact that women played a prominent part in glossolalia, explains why this injunction appears just here. As to the underlying principle, we can only repeat what we said about xi. 2-16. Paul emphasizes in conclusion: (we must revert to xii. 1) what has been said must be regarded as the commandments of the Lord (verse 37). Whoever is a real prophet or "pneumatic" will understand that. Hence, we are not dealing with an incidental criticism, not with benevolent injunctions, but with a last word that is to be said in all of them. Paul ventures to employ the Either-Or: if any man does not know this, then is he, too, not known. Whoever does not know here, is not known (in the sense of viii. 3; xiii. 12; xv. 34), and does not know what God, what revelation is. An utterly disquieting word, a disturbing, self-conscious one-sidedness, or, as one must say, a strange shooting of sparrows with cannon, if Paul was here really only concerned with that of which he was speaking, prophecy and glossolalia, comprehensible only when it is realized how all these things are for him transparent, only an occasion to bear his apostolic testimony by constantly pointing away from this foreground to a quite other background, only, therefore, if he really, throughout the Epistle, not only criticizes and corrects this and that, but, in passing by this and that, wants, at any rate, to confront the Church with a last question and decision.

§ 9

Before we approach chapter xv. let us endeavour once more to visualize the meaning of the road we have travelled, the continuity of the Epistle. Can we speak of a meaning at all? Can the contents of the Epistle be brought within a common denominator? *First,* in chapters i.-iv. Paul, in connexion with the Christian gnosticism prevalent among the Corinthian religious parties, called attention to the fact that gnosis in Christianity could not signify anything else than insight into the reversal of all things, which lies in the fact that the subject of real wisdom is not man but God, and that gnosis can only exist in the recognition of this incomprehensible inversion: "from God." *Secondly,* in chapters v.-vi., with respect to the outbreaks of unbridled vitality, he reminded his readers that man in Christianity is absolutely no longer his own master, but is confiscated in his creaturehood as God's property, and that this signifies a crisis which he can no longer escape. *Thirdly,* in chapter vii., sharply veering round and *in concreto* (the question is the permissibility of marriage), he made it clear, even against his personal opinion, that the "from God" applies critically even to the conduct of life that is opposed to libertinism, to asceticism, the appeal to God, which is a special one for each man, as a limitation imposed even upon arbitrary striving after purity. *Fourthly,* in chapters viii.-x., against the freedom based on Christian knowledge as properly understood, he asserts, towards the weak brother, that which is really lawful, the love that edifies, the glory of God as the standard against which even well-founded individualism is measured in Christianity, as the enigma which must stand in the way even of the greatest truth and clarity, if they are not, on reaching their summit, to turn into lies. *Fifthly,* in chapter xi., he cast his protection over the Christian morals threatened with corruption, by his energetic reminder of the object of Christian divine service, which is a judgment upon the latter, when human arrogance, be it of a male or female kind, usurps the place which the reverence and humility of all should occupy. *Sixthly,* in chapters xii.-xiv., he finally hurled into the manifold arbitrary development of spiritual gifts the critical idea of unity and order, which are given in order that these should be understood as God's gifts, which confer upon the gifted one, as such, no special right whatever, not even towards his differently endowed fellows, which rather, just because of the different endowment of his fellow men, show each one in his limitations, which he is then also to recognize as the limitations imposed on him by God. How the peak-point of chapter xiii., with its sudden reference to the love that never ceases, to the reality which exists beyond all the crises, and whence all the crises come, soars above this plain, we have seen. Upon the basis of this analysis, I believe I am justified in my opinion that chapters i.-xiv. of the First Epistle to the Corinthians form *really* a *whole.* The disparateness of the subjects with which he deals, the frequent obscurity of the personal and contemporary details, finally, the absolute limitation of the substance of

his speech, thoughts, and ideas by the time (in this
respect as much can be conceded to the historians
as they want to claim), none of this, if we emphatically inquire: what is he really speaking of? can
prevent us from hearing the *cantus firmus,* from
seeing the "red thread" which runs through the
whole. The sole, or at any rate vital, assumption
which I make, is that when Paul spoke of God (from
the side of God, from God, to God's glory), he really
meant *God,* and that it is permissible, even imperative, and from this standpoint, to interpret all his
ideas, however they may otherwise be historically
and psychologically determined, to take him at his
word, calculating that all his utterances, however
ambiguous they may be regarded within the realm of
history, relate, beyond the realm of history, unequivocally to God, and that this relationship gives
to everything its peculiar concrete meaning, however little we are able to ascertain this everywhere
with equal distinctness. If this supposition is right,
it is further to be said, that the essential unity of the
First Epistle to the Corinthians is a quite specific
criticism which Paul applies to the Christian Church.
He reproaches it with the fact that the human, the
vital, the heroic or even colossal, the individual
arbitrary elements, which are mixed up in its Christianity, as in every other human phenomenon, are
in process of growing with rank luxuriance, and
becoming an end in themselves. Amid the full
self-understood recognition of God, Christ, and the
Holy Ghost, in the full enjoyment of a great
Christian religious estate, they are in process of
becoming a "Christian world." They are going on

far too well. Christianity was flourishing in Corinth in a disquieting fashion. A Kingdom-of-God's springtime seems to have been dawning there, such as was hardly to be recorded subsequently in the best ages of revival. If we were not accustomed from of yore to regard Christian Corinth in the light of what Paul found to *censure,* instead of, and first of all, in the light of what Paul expressly and positively valued, we should appraise the conditions which the Epistle illuminates quite differently, and also better understand the attitude of Paul. Paul sees in these conditions man rearing himself up— Christian man, but *man* nevertheless—rearing himself up against *God.* And in this he now perceives not only a danger, but plainly *the* danger. For what is at stake in Christianity is the rule of God and nothing else. That is the Either-Or with which he confronts the Corinthian Church all along the line. He exhorts them to return to their right minds, to go back to the beginning; he tells them in ever new words, upon ever fresh occasions: it won't do! He reminds them incessantly of the last things, which in Christianity are emphatically the first. That he does this in polemical spirit, in the analysis of perfectly definite Christian phenomena, although with the thoughtful goodness and calm of a father, imparts its special colouring to the First Epistle to the Corinthians. There stands Paul, and behind him a mountain-high, marvellous secret, and he points his finger to what passes under the name of Christianity in Corinth: and then he stands again by the side of the Corinthian Christians, and once more points his finger, but now back to the place whence he was speaking a moment before. In this thence and thither consists the critical and polemical element of the First Epistle to the Corinthians. It is well to realize that this thence and thither is the most positive thing that there is, but we must also be perfectly clear that it did not, at first at any rate, have this effect, and is not calculated to have this effect upon us in the ordinary way. It was addressed to the Church of Corinth, and whoever read this Epistle must have been completely upset and shattered. What then remains after all these repudiations, restrictions, and warnings? Must not this Epistle have had the effect of an earthquake, which would render any remaining ordered Church life impossible? Whence comes all the simplicity which seems to us essential to right Christianity if such a crisis breaks in, and, indeed, issues from the venerated founder of the Church, who points to its positive divine source? We may ask whether the Epistle must not also have upon us at first a merely shattering effect, exciting doubt, confusion, uncertainty, if the matter were not so inexpressibly far removed from us, if we were not in the habit of remembering extracts from such of the chief sayings as are to some extent illuminating and usable, such as, for instance, i. 18, 30; ii. 9, 10; iii., 11; iv., 20; vi., 20; x., 13, and, of course, chapter xiii. But these outstanding passages torn from their context are *not* the First Epistle to the Corinthians. The First Epistle to the Corinthians as a whole, as it stands, is a weighty attack upon Christianity, much more drastic than, for example, the penitential sermon of the Epistle of James, more drastic, at any rate, than what Kierkegaard said under that head. A not unimportant part of its effect surely consists in the fact that Paul continually included himself in the question and placed himself under the judgment. Hence, he can extend his reach thus far and scarcely leave a refuge for the Corinthian Church. There is also another thing to be said: if one should propose to talk about the so-called absoluteness of the so-called Christian religion, perhaps the best thing to do would be to point out that such a self-criticism as this was possible at any rate in the beginning, and to ask whether such a line of thought as is visible in 1 Cor. i.-xiv. can also be traced in any Greek document? A negative index, at least a shadow, or perhaps the reflexion of a primeval light of unparalleled brightness, seems to be visible in this thoroughgoing self-criticism of the young Christianity, *which to be sure, does not lend itself to apologetic purposes,* but which, in certain circumstances, would force attention to the problem of revelation and of the absolute. It remains a remarkable fact that, out of the Greek confusion of religions, just *this* religion, which was capable of self-criticism, emerged comparatively victorious and superior.

II

THE RESURRECTION CHAPTER

IT cannot be by chance that 1 Cor. xv., the chapter which deals with the most positive subject that can be imagined, forms the very peak and crown of this essentially critical and polemically negative Epistle. What is disclosed here is Paul's key position. The Resurrection of the Dead is the point from which Paul is speaking and to which he points. From this standpoint, not only the death of those now living, but, above all, their life *this side* of the threshold of death, is in the apostolic sermon, veritably seen, understood, judged, and placed in the light of the last severity, the last hope. Our deliberations so far have shown us what Paul understood by this: to place the life of man in its heights and depths in the light of the great answer which answers all his questions—exactly on the threshold of death. The great answer which, by reason of the fact that it is exactly given *there,* first awakens all the questions of life, comprehends in a single great question, can only confront mankind as the question of all questions, and in this disguise as question can only be grasped as answer also. 1 Cor. xv. contains the doctrine of the *last things.*

In using this expression we involuntarily think of

events and figures belonging to a future of the world, of humanity and the individual, which is wrapped in obscurity, which is perhaps immediately imminent, but perhaps thousands upon thousands of years distant from us in time; we think of "the end of history" in the sense of the termination of history, history at the termination of the story, of the life story of the individual as well as the story of the world and of the Church, in fact, even of natural history, in a possibility beyond those known to us, but always as new, unknown further possibilities linking up with the latter in continuous succession, although perhaps amid unparalleled catastrophes, surpassing and perpetuating them upon a higher plane. Why should there not be "ends of history" and "last things" in this sense too? Why should it not be deserving of serious consideration? The endeavours that abound in all epochs and civilizations, never successfully suppressed but never wholly without any success at all, to penetrate the secret of continual existence in time, forbid us to leave entirely out of our calculations a calm consideration, at any rate of this, according as one regards it, joyful or melancholy possibility. There might be something in it. Why not?

Further, the great historical transformations, whence we have emerged, and in the midst of which we are standing, the supposition which can hardly be kept out of sight, that entirely different things might be in store for our so-called civilized world in the near or remote future, facilitate our appreciation of the possibility that a final term of history, although perhaps for a time only in the form of a new ice age,

such as plays an important part (really not un-
merited) in Troeltsch's theology, might dawn upon
the whole. And if the extinguishing of a star in the
dark firmament accidentally reminds us that somewhere, at a distance which we are quite unable to
apprehend or imagine, a world has actually and
literally perished and been dissolved into its atoms,
it may be decades or centuries ago, so the consideration that far away and long ago such a thing happened is, at any rate, less ingenious than the other,
which is obvious to an unsophisticated mind *iam
proximus ardet Ucalegon* (Virgil's "Now neighbour
Ucalegon is on fire") such a thing might happen to
us even to-day. As images of "last things," such
final possibilities, lying so far and yet so near us,
might well be instructive and stimulating, especially
if we should unhappily be indifferent to the obvious
symbols of "last things," ice ages, and the fate of
expiring worlds in the past and the present, by
which we are, without resort to metempsychosis,
surrounded.

But "last things," in the sense of 1 Cor. xv. and
in the sense of the New Testament generally, are *not*
such final possibilities, however real they may seem
to our eyes. Not even if we conceive them only as
preliminary stages to physical-metaphysical, cosmic-
metacosmic transformations and revolutions of an
unparalleled kind. Not even if the picture of this
background of history's end is composed of, and constructed with, material taken from the Bible and
perhaps even from 1 Cor. xv. "Everything transi-
tory" is only a parable; that even the objects of the
biblical world of apprehension belong to the passing;

that they are meant to serve and not to rule, to signify and not to be, the Bible, at any rate, leaves us in no doubt. Last *things,* as such, are not *last* things, however great and significant they may be. He only speaks of *last* things who would speak of the *end* of all things, of their end understood plainly and fundamentally, of a reality so radically superior to all things, that the existence of all things would be utterly and entirely *based* upon it alone, and thus, in speaking of their end, he would in truth be speaking of nothing else than their beginning. And when he speaks of history-end and of time-end, he is only speaking of the *end* of history and the *end* of time. But once more of its end, understood thus fundamentally, thus plainly, of a reality so radically superior to all happening and all temporality, that in speaking of the finiteness of history and the finiteness of time, he is also speaking of that upon which all time and all happening is *based.* The end of history must be for him synonymous with the pre-history, the limits of time of which he speaks must be the limits of all and every time and thus necessarily the *origin* of time.

The representations of "last things" or of "end-of-history" engrafted upon the language and world of apprehension of the Bible have, however primitive they may be in certain circumstances, at least the great advantage over other similar things, that the idea of eternity, at least according to name and place, is not quite unknown to them. The "last things," however weightily they may be arranged in sequence, the final-history, with whatever complications it may be spun out, here become, willy-nilly, the end of all things, the end of history, so far as, where the idea of eternity is not quite unknown, the real end at last, the absorption of all this and that, all here and there, all once and now into the solemn peace of the One, is found to occur at a definite place. Here, if this idea in its justifying power is even to some extent known, one is at any rate preserved from plunging like a drunkard into the bottomless abyss of a supposed absolute future, and, like the eternal Jew, if not wandering among, at any rate pondering upon, the succession of millions of years, or even the succession of æons, and to regard the result of this as eschatology. Somehow and somewhere the infinite series is apt to come to a stop in a thought somehow determined by the Bible, the infinite series thus becoming a finite one, in view of the insurmountable wall which is placed against it by the eternity where God is all in all. Here it cannot be altogether forgotten and overlooked that the eternity, of which others perhaps also speak, is the eternity of *God,* that is to say, the *rule,* the *Kingdom* of God, His absolute *transcendence* as Creator, Redeemer, and King of things, of history; thus not just the infinity of the world of time, of things, above all of men, but, however it may stand with the due prolongation of their existence into a beyond, their fundamental finiteness. The force of this biblical idea of eternity is to-day sustaining such a man as Kuno Fiedler with his passionate gospel of the "Dawn of Nihilism."

But here we may not stop half-way. The knowledge that it is God's eternity which sets a limit to the endlessness of the world, of time, of things, of

men, must be made fruitful. The *last* word that is
spoken here must be so understood as last word that
it can at the same time be understood as *first* word,
the history of the end at the same time, and, as
such, the history of the beginning—as the first word,
and as the history of the beginning of all time, of the
whole of time, of the oldest ages as well as of the
latest ages, and of all the ages situated at the centre.
Time as such is finite by virtue of its limitation by
eternity. But as the word that first establishes and
as the history of the beginning it must be understood, as the word and history of the origin of all
time, of the whole of time. For if eternity limits and
sets an end to time as such, it marks it indeed as
finite, but it *marks* it. Whoever clearly grasps this
is removed from the temptation to confuse the end-
of-history with a termination of history, however
impressive and wonderful it may be. Of the *real*
end-of-history it may be said at any time: The end
is near! Even of an age of the greatest and most impressive catastrophes of the most supernatural kind
only this could be said fundamentally: The end is
near! and that applies fundamentally also to yester-
day, to-day, and to-morrow. But he will also be removed from the other temptation, to confuse eternity
with a great annihilation, and to make of the end-of-
history an annihilation of history. That would, in
fact, not be real eternity, not even the eternity of
God, which dissolves time into infinity, instead of
marking it (*marking it*) as infinite. A thinker who
obeys wholly and not only in part the promptings of
the Bible, then, must pass right through these two
temptations. The doctrine of "last things" or

eschatology is, therefore, unless this conception is very thoroughly explained, a misleading, and, in any case, inadequate description of what Paul expounded in 1 Cor. xv.

If the assumption is correct upon which we have so far proceeded in our commentary, that the discourse of the apostle in the whole Epistle proceeds from a single point and harks back again to this same point, and that 1 Cor. xv. is to be understood as an attempt to express in words this one single point in itself, severed from the relationships in which it had up till now almost only been visible, then the doctrine of the Resurrection of the Dead which he expounds here is in no case an "eschatology" in the sense which attaches to this word in ordinary dogma, that is, an attempt, after speaking of everything else possible, to bring forward something about death, the beyond and world perfection, but we have to do here with the doctrine of the "End," which is at the same time the beginning, of the last things, which are, at the same time, the first. The chapter treats of Death and the Dead, in sharp contrast to the abundance of the possibilities of life which was the theme of chapter xiv. All those things which the Corinthian Christians were previously bidden to lay to heart suddenly appear here in the pale light of the fact that they must die. Truly, this is not a recollection among other recollections: it is *the* recollection which Paul wants to awaken. But the theme is to be the *resurrection* of the dead. Only that gives meaning and emphasis to the recollection. What is the end, if it be only the end? What is eternity, if it be only eternity? What can touch us,

when we are *not,* when we do not know, when we
cannot have?   With the word "resurrection," however, the apostolic preaching puts in this empty place
against all that exists for us, all that is known to us,
all that can be possessed by us, all things of all time
—what? not the non-being, the unknown, the not-to-
be-possessed, nor yet a second being, a further thing
to become known, a higher future possession, but the
source and the truth of all that exists, that is known,
that can belong to us, the reality of all *res,* of all
things, the eternity of time, the *resurrection* of the
dead.   But be it understood: all this exactly in that
empty place, and therefore exactly where only the
indifferent conception of the non-existent, unknown,
inconceivable seems to have room, where only the
dissolution of all things and phenomena seems to be
in question, where only the contradictory assertion
of the infinity of time seems to be left, where death
seems to be the last word.   The dead: that is what
we are.   The risen: that is what we are not.   But
precisely for this reason the resurrection of the dead
involves that that which *we are not* is equivalent
with that which *we are*: the dead living, time
eternity, the being truth, things real.   All this is not
given except in hope, and therefore this identity is
not to be put into effect.   The life that we dead are
living here and now is not, therefore, to be confounded with *this* life, of which we can only ever say
that we are not yet living in it; the endlessness of
time is not to be confused with eternity; the corporeality of phenomena is not to be confused with
this reality; the being that we know or can know is
not to be confused with *this* its origin, in its truth;

the sharp, fundamental step which parts the latter
from the former, as the impossible from the possible,
is not to be removed, but *given* in hope—in hope, in
the identification of the former with the latter, the
resurrection of the dead already *effected* in God.
This is what is behind the recollection of the fact
that we must die, which here at the end of the Epistle
finally appears on the scene after casting its shadow
widely enough before. The recollection of death is
so important, so urgent, so disturbing, so actual because it is in fact really the tidings of the resurrection behind it, the recollection of the *life,* of our life
that we are not living and that yet is our life. Hence
the end of the Epistle is also its beginning, its principle that supports and actuates the whole, because it
is not only a termination, but the end.

The ideas developed in 1 Cor. xv. could be better
described as the *methodology of the apostle's preaching,* rather than eschatology, because it is really concerned not with this and that special thing, but with
the meaning and nerve of its whole, with the whence?
and the whither? of the human way as such and in
itself. A dangerous simplification of the problem!
Can we speak of it as such, isolated? The question
applies to all methodology. Can we say even a
single appropriate, really enlightening word about
assumptions as such, abstracted from their applica-
tions to any sphere whatsoever? Can we draw the
bird on the wing? Would we not then be drawing
something quite different, that is to say, at best a
series of instantaneous pictures, of which not a
single one in itself really reproduces the flying bird?
Are we not in every individual word and utterance

speaking in fact of the dead, when we mean the most living?   Even if the speaker is called Paul?   Undoubtedly, I would make answer.   Undoubtedly, the attempt that is made here, the attempt to utter the *impossible,* and to that extent a wholly impossible attempt, in which one is apt to run into a heavy fog, is exposed to extreme misunderstanding, even if one's name is Paul.   To how many misunderstandings has 1 Cor. xv. been exposed from of yore!   How infinitely cautious must we be here, if we are to understand, proceeding step by step, if we are to avoid straying to the right or the left into meaningless platitudes or into utterly hopeless obscurity: into ideas out of which no way of knowledge leads either forward or backward.   How tempting it is to read verses 3-11, for example, with the eyes of historical intelligence, whereby it would make a small difference to the infertility of the yield whether one was resolved to deny or recognize the so-called miracle.   What a bad heteronomy of faith and of obedience can be gathered from verses 12-34, where instead of upon their own freedom, both are based apparently so unequivocally upon a third and fourth, upon a historical event, and in the light of the beyond!   Are not verses 35-49 typical speculative metaphysics and apologetics?   And finally, are not verses 50-57 quite characteristically one of those end-of-histories which are no end-of-histories at all, but only the unparalleled continuations of history?

Moreover, it does not amount to much whether one's attitude is one of positive agreement, either out of conviction or out of respect for the Bible, or one of rejection, or, as is probably the case with most, one of mere sceptical marvelling at all of it. Paul must have had his special intention—an *ultima ratio* against this particular Church—in daring to make this impossible attempt in such detail, and offering so many weak points. Otherwise, he would have done it only incidentally and summarily. There are reasons why this chapter in Pauline literature, although threads can be drawn through it in all directions, stands *alone* as the connected exposition of this truth. Such a thing as this was not said every day. Was it inevitable that in the Corinthian Church, with the many penultimate words that were known, listened to, and uttered there, the last word was now declared once for all, in manner unprecedented? It almost seems so. For the rest, however, it must be said that the impossible attempt to say *that,* the word of all words, is nothing else than the essence of the apostolic preaching generally. All the time, the question in the *background* is concerning *this* God, *this* Christ, *this* Holy Ghost, this *last* word. The difficulties, misunderstandings, and ambiguities with which we see Paul surrounded here are those that surround the Christian testimony as such, as surely as it is a testimony of divine truth given in human speech, except that here they emerge with the testimony itself from the background of announcement into the foreground, and are thus more conspicuous. This chapter is admirably suited to clarify what Christianity as a whole involves, and to provoke a salutary shock at the fact that theology really signifies an enterprise which is impossible to man, owing to the expository detail in which Paul shows this to us. Whether all the obvious misunder-

standings can still perchance be avoided, whether it
is possible, despite all the difficulties, not only to
understand the individual thoughts of the apostle,
but, and upon this everything depends, to *follow* the
movement of his thoughts from afar and to hear
with more or less distinctness the most vital things
which he intended to say and yet nowhere can say—
all this we must now show. Let us be prepared for
partial failure from the start. We are probably (and
not only historically) too far away from Paul to be
able to approach him here, even approximately.

Lastly, taking a retrospective view of the contents
of this Epistle which we have hitherto discussed,
and glancing at what has just been said, let us consider the following preliminary details from the
chapter itself: verses 1-2 are the strong expression
of Paul's opinion that in what followed he was saying to them *nothing* that was *in any way new* or special, no esoteric secret doctrine, no special Paulinism, but simply reminding them of the basis of their
Christianity, not to summon them elsewhere, but to
call them back to themselves. "So far as you do
not believe in vain, you believe this and that," such
and such is the meaning and content and truth of
your faith, is what he means. That he is not of
opinion that the resurrection of the dead should be
announced as a partial and special truth, but as *the*
truth, is shown, apart from the weighty severity
which pervades this chapter more even than the
preceding chapters, by the description of what he
means as the *gospel* plainly (verse 1). What is
involved is the *substance*, the *whole* of the Christian
revelation. It was *not a theological doubt,* to be cor-

rected incidentally or even overlooked, but an attack upon what made Christianity to be Christianity in the case of those who said "there is no resurrection of the dead" (verse 12); thus what was involved was not a doctrinal dispute, although the attack is expressed in the form of a false doctrine. After all that we have heard from Paul himself about the Christianity of those in Corinth, we have no alternative but to believe that the resurrection was denied there. If that were not the case, then the whole Epistle would not have been written, or needed to be written, in such a manner. Where the situation resembled that in Corinth, the resurrection was denied, no matter whether the false doctrine was expressly set up or not. The "some among you" of verse 12, who had just stated frankly their position, are certainly by no means the worst, on the contrary, perhaps even the most honest, and in so far the most hopeful persons, with whom one can at any rate argue, because they have at least gone so far as openly to avow their denial of the gospel upon which the Church was founded. Whereas the others, whose thoughts, lives, and characters appeared equally dubious from the standpoint of this gospel, might perhaps have made shift with mediating attempts and illusions. Even considered superficially it is still hardly to be supposed that Paul would have written the whole of this detailed exposition merely to "some among you" or on their account, but Paul must somehow, consciously or unconsciously, have seen the whole Church standing behind them and solidly with them. In the absence of the phrase of verse 12 "some among you say," the rest of the chapter would not, at any rate, warrant the assumption that it was concerned with a theological heresy on the part of a *few*, but everything points to the fact that everything is said more or less directly to the whole Church, of whom the "certain among you" seem more like *select representatives*. Additional weight is also lent to this supposition by the fact that Paul nowhere makes any personal complaint against the persons in question, nowhere demands that even disciplinary action should be taken against them, that the usual title of "brethren" (verses 1, 31, 50, 58) is addressed to all readers, without exception, and that he even calls them, verse 31, as well as the Thessalonians and Philippians, his "glory in Christ."

But the establishment of this fact, with which we embark upon a special consideration of the chapter, must not deter us from attempting, by means of the material offered by the chapter itself, to construct a picture of the contradiction which, according to verse 12, was formally levelled in Corinth, at, we will say, the "Pauline" gospel; a picture of the methodistic antagonism in which the "certain among you," however many or few were behind them, found themselves to the gospel of Paul. This picture may be inferred with reasonable clearness from Paul's rejoinder. They, the doubters, are manifestly quite unconscious that their thoughts and speech have the range which Paul ascribes to them. They have heard, assented to, and accepted, the gospel preached by Paul in Corinth, his *kerygma* (verses 14-15), but they obviously take a certain exception to it, inasmuch as they aver that such gospel, viz. the gospel preached by *him*, Paulinism, is not identical with the plain gospel, and not alone decisive, but is to be treated selectively (verses 8-11). The objection with which Paul had to deal in these verses was paraphrased by Luther in the following words (in which he was certainly in the main on the right track): "The factious spirits behaved towards him as they always do when they said to him: 'Is the Holy Ghost such a poor beggar that He can find nobody except Paul?' just as they are now saying: 'Are they at Wittenberg, then, alone so wise? is no one else to know anything? and cannot the Spirit also be among us?' What do they know more than we?" (Erlangen Ed., xix. 107).

Thus the objection which is dealt with here is one that is really illuminating to our own minds. The doubters are in agreement with Paul that Christianity is concerned with the salvation of men (verse 2), and they are perfectly conscious of holding the faith (verses 2, 14, 17), faith in the forgiveness of sins (verses 3, 17, 34? 56?). Obviously, they affirm in a most vigorous manner the supernatural reality of baptism (verse 29). They are emphatically not Epicureans, but on the contrary are inclined towards a strict morality (verses 32, 33), they have desire and understanding for the grandeur of martyrdom (verses 30-32); in fact, they exert themselves for the works of the Lord, that is, obviously for the victory of His cause, verse 58. But, they say also, the restriction, or the deduction which they fancy they are obliged to make from Paulinism, is just this: why is the resurrection of the dead required to be accepted by all? (verse 12). It is not as if the resurrection of Christ from the dead were perchance disputed, they affirmed it (verses 13, 16), but they regarded it as an isolated historical event, which did *not*, at any rate, stand to us in the relationship that upon the basis thereof our own resurrection must be affirmed (verse 15). They believe and affirm also that those who had fallen asleep in Christ were not lost (verse 18), that, therefore, there was a continued existence after death in a somehow conceivable beyond. But obviously they regarded this "beyond" somehow as a prolongation of *this* life, for only in *this* life have they hope in Christ (verse 19). For them the Kingdom of God does not fall outside the sphere of flesh and blood; to seek and to find incorruption in corruption does not appear to them to be at all impossible; but they see in it the very Christian possibility "to be eternal in every moment" (verse 50). To them death is something inevitable which overtakes man, all men must die (verse 51). It is not an enemy, let alone the "last enemy" (verse 26); it is not the decisive question with which man is confronted, let alone the place where he must give the decisive answer! For them the overcoming of *sins* is not inseparably connected with a victory over death, they do not perceive why this victory should be *the* victory (verses 54-57). That by resurrection, anything else than *bodily* resurrection could be understood by Paul or by the doubters is an assumption to be found nowhere throughout the chapter. It goes without saying that bodily resurrection is meant. Hence they stumble against this very obstacle. It is just here that Christian monism dashes itself in vain against the discontinuity, against the dialectic of Pauline thought, against the No, which in its gospel of their hope in Christ they set against this life. Continued existence after death, which they also accept, must still be only a spiritual, an immaterial existence! Why? Well, of course, so that it might find a place in a satisfactory, comprehensive philosophy beside this present bodily life. A soul which lives on after death may, at least, be plausibly asserted, if not perhaps demonstrated, without disturbing the picture of world uniformity. But the resurrection of the body, this same body that we plainly see dying and perishing, the assertion, therefore, not of a duality of life here and life to come, but of an identity of the two, not given now, not to be directly ascertained, but only to be hoped for, only to be believed in, this is manifestly nothing but the ruthless destruction of that unity, a "scandal," irrationality, and religious materialism. Whether it be felt as harshly as this, it remains the same. *This is the "scandal," stumbling-block, in question.*

The objection raised against Paul, formulated with somewhat less severity, is summarized very well in the explanatory words of W. Bousset, in which he aims at clarifying, not the attitude of the Corinthian doubters of the resurrection, but his own attitude towards the chapter: "The most important, the central element of the hope of Paul, to which he clings with all the ardour of his soul, is the expectation of a new 'pneumatic' body. The emphasis which Paul places on this aspect of the Christian hope would seem almost strange to us. For us the most important and glorious part of the Christian hope seems to consist in the certitude of the continuation of personal life beyond death and the grave. For us everything else, even the question of a new body, is at least obscure and doubtful. And the idea of the great act of the end of the world and the general resurrection lies for us at the most only at the periphery of our thinking." The Corinthian doubters, at any rate, do not agree with us here. Just at this point occurs their protesting question: "How are the dead raised up? and with what body do they come?" (verse 35), and whoever else does not agree with us here may take it as an indication that 1 Cor. xv. was also written against, or rather for, him. But merely as an indication! The dispute about the corporeality of the resurrection is also nothing more than an index of the clash of much deeper and more extensive antagonisms. Just try with the eyes of the doubters of 1 Cor. xv., so far as their views are clear to us here, to read, say, Rom. iii.-viii. Could Rom. v. 12-21, with its conception of death and its unrighteous rule coming through sin in the world, be understood from this point of view? Or Rom. vi. 2-11, the indissoluble connexion between the overcoming of sin and death by the death and resurrection of Christ? Or Rom. iii. 9-20, the impossibility of being just before God in the flesh? Or Rom. i. 17-22, the purely promissory character of faith? Or Rom. vii. 14-25, the deadly captivity of natural man outside the communion with the risen proclaimed in Rom. viii. 1? Or Rom. viii. 9-11, the Spirit as the force which calls a new corporeality into existence? Or Rom. viii. 19-23, the unity not of the godless, but of the very children of God with

the need of the fallen creation? Or Romans viii.
24-25: "By hope we are saved"? And how many
other passages could be quoted from this Epistle
alone? Whatever attitude we may adopt towards
Paul, it must at least be obvious from the first glance
that, in dealing with the Corinthian doubters, he was
not concerned with this thing or that thing, but with
the *whole*.

The point at which such a dispute breaks out, here
the corporeality of the resurrection, is always something strange to spectators who overlook what is
involved. They are accustomed to think that the
dispute upon this point relates to the Nicæan question of consubstantiality, to the *hoc est corpus
Meum*, the "this is My body" of the Lord's Supper
controversy, to the quarrels about oblates, baptismal
fonts and brides' veils, owing to which Calvin was
expelled from Geneva in 1536, and complain about
pettiness and hair-splitting. But the onlookers must
first acquire the competence to judge such questions
by proving that they could do better, if they were
not just onlookers. In the controversy over the
resurrection, two worlds clash (the question of
corporeality is only the extreme point at which they
touch); the world of the gospel (let us repeat: as
Paul understands it), and a religious and moral
world which looks very much like Christianity,
which, undoubtedly, has its eminent qualities and
excellencies, in which many alleged and also many
real Paulinists would have to notice all kinds of
things worthy of reflection and imitation, which certainly signifies a possibility of thinking, of speaking,
and of living that is very respectable, that requires

no apology for its existence, and that demands very calm and real judgment—the world whence, at any rate, not only the Corinthians, but we with them, whatever may be our attitude towards the question in dispute, always come. Nevertheless, the conflict is first brought to a head over the question of the conception of what we are accustomed to call the Beyond.

May I formulate what the doubters of 1 Cor. xv. desired and represented in the words of another expositor, whose conception of the matter is akin to mine? Friedrich Zündel wrote that what was involved was "the attempt to eliminate from the whole organism of the substance of belief the hope of the resurrection of the dead as something superfluous, as an unnecessary strain placed upon so-called reason. The Corinthians probably began simply to console themselves with the hope of dying blessed in the name of Jesus, and the rest—as they might say —to leave confidently to God. Hence there began, on the one hand, that unfortunate breaking up of what we call Christianity into individualism [Zündel means going to heaven in the narrow personal sense and wanting to be blessed in contrast to the hope of God's universal kingdom], and, on the other hand, that falsehood borrowed from paganism by virtue of which our actual situation would no longer be judged according to the testimony of hard reality, but according to an alleged faith, that is, a wanton play of the imagination with respect to the invisible. The pagan falsehood at the base of it is the contempt of visible reality and the manner of ascribing to the divine only the sphere of the invisible, and there bespeaking a good seat, off one's own bat, as it were. With what holy pride the apostle protests against the view that he leads such a hard life for the sake of such illusions, and with what victorious pride he lays claim to the whole of tangible reality in the name of his Lord Jesus."

We may find this description of the opponent, that is, of the Corinthian Christianity with which Paul here grapples in a decisive struggle, to be a caricature. It is notorious that caricatures reproduce the essentials of a face frequently better than photographs. If the face of the Corinthian doubters of the resurrection, in Zündel's description, should perhaps seem more familiar to you than previously, notably recalling something which we know by no means as heresy, but as ecclesiastical Christianity, you will, I should say, have seen what is historically real and true. This also harmonizes with what I said at the outset, that these good people were not in the least aware of the extent of their antagonism to Paul. They saw the antagonism only on the one point, which from their point of view was merely a theological difference, respecting which a different opinion might reasonably be held without calling Christianity as such into question. They merely took offence, as Lietzmann believes, at the Jewish doctrine of the resurrection, from the standpoint of the Greek belief in immortality, or as Bousset suggests: at the unconscious compromise between the Jewish and the Greek conception of the future life, within which Paul moved, but for the rest obviously did not dream of unravelling the antagonism between themselves and Paul in its fundamental acuteness. They thought: "here we cannot agree with you," and did not even suspect that they failed to agree with Paul generally. Just as one may read in many modern books dealing with this and similar passages from Paul: here Paul is foreign and obscure to us, or if intelligible, he is unacceptable, or if acceptable, indifferent, without those who write in this strain appearing to be aware of the fact that they are at the same time confessing that Paul as a whole is in truth obscure, unacceptable or indifferent to them.

This brings us back once more for a short time to the position of Paul himself. Paul did not describe all his ideas and declarations as undiscussible *conditiones sine quibus non* of Christianity, and, where he did so, it was with a varying emphasis. That he did this here with the greatest emphasis can scarcely admit of any doubt. It is he, not the Corinthian doubters, who brings out the fundamental antagonism to its sharpest expression. Jewish doctrine of the resurrection, or compromising eschatology here or there—what has previously been said respecting the limitation of Pauline thought by the conditions of the time also applies here—to ascertain this much does not advance our real understanding by a single step. This much is certain, that Paul here saw threatened in the most vital point, not only himself, but the gospel, the work of the Lord (verse 58) in which the Corinthians indeed also took part in their way, and from which he did not exclude them in telling them the truth. We are, of course, perfectly free, before and after, to hold another opinion respecting even this solemn protest of Paul, that is, as Bousset, for example, candidly admits, to perceive in the opinion of his Corinthian opponents *nothing* of vital menace, *nothing* of the fundamental antagonism of two worlds, but *only* a theological difference, a remote quarrel between a Pharisee and a number of Greeks. Why should we not be permitted to understand the gospel quite differently from Paul, passing quite by Paul's interrogative position? But in that case his solemn protest must become perfectly clear to us, inasmuch as if we part from him here we part from him *generally*. It will not do to reject Paul here, whilst finding his words in Rom. viii. 28 or 1 Cor. xiii. marvellously true and edifying; for if we reject him here we prove that we have understood even Rom. viii. 28 and 1 Cor. xiii. quite differently from him; he himself says emphatically that he desires to be understood from this standpoint. Paul says as distinctly as possible that the contradiction which he sees facing him here touches the basis upon which the Church stands "wherein ye stand; by which also ye are saved" (verses 1-2). He raises the question whether the faith of the doubters and of the Church is not "void," "vain," "empty" (verses 14, 17). It is a matter of ignorance (verse 34), not, as in viii. 7, of an ignorance such as that of the Pauline doctrine of freedom, which can at any rate be tolerated, but of the utterly intolerable ignorance of God. "Certain people have even no inkling of God," is Bousset's excellent translation of this passage. The nerve of Christianity is, in Paul's view, severed if the Corinthians think that flesh and blood can inherit the Kingdom of God, corruption inherit incorruption. Cannot inherit! says Paul. "Now this I say . . . *cannot*" (verse 50).

The First Epistle to the Corinthians is written from the standpoint of this "not," nay, from that of the most positive thing that exists, which looms behind, and that is the very Resurrection of the Dead with which this chapter deals, indeed, fairly summarily in four sections, which I would divide and paraphrase in the simplest words as follows: Verses 1-11, The Message of the Resurrection as the Foundation of the Church. Verses 13-34, The Resurrection as the Meaning of Faith. Verses 35-49, The Resurrection as Truth. Verses 50-58, The Resurrection as Actuality.

III

EXPLANATION OF I CORINTHIANS XV

§ 1

The Resurrection Gospel as the Foundation of the Church (vs. 1-11)

"Moreover, breathren, I declare unto you the gospel which I preached unto you, which also ye have received, and wherein ye stand; by which also ye are saved, if ye keep in memory what I preached unto you, unless ye have believed in vain."—vs. 1, 2.

THE meaning of the whole section, and equally of these first verses, is the intention to make the readers realize that the critical assumption of the Epistle, which is now expressly to be mentioned, is not a personal sentiment or opinion or tendency of Paul; nothing strange, but what is closest and most familiar to themselves; nothing new, but the old; nothing accidental and peripheral, but the foundation and the centre, by virtue of which they are Christians. Hence, "I declare [make known] unto you." (I call to your remembrance.) The one assumption upon which this intention is based is that the readers are no longer or are not yet settled (verse 58), are *unsure* in their standing upon their own basis; the other, subsequently developed, that, although unsure, they are actually *standing* thereon, and therefore all that is needed is a call to remembrance. This superior confidence of Paul in the impregnable power of what established the Church must, from the outset, be kept in view, with special reference to verse 58. It is not truth that is threatened, but men in their relation to truth. Paul was the messenger who communicated this fundamental gospel to them. This imposed on him the duty and gave him the right to recall to them, to ask them what they made of that which he did not give them, but communicated to them. He feels responsible, less for them than for the shape which the matter has assumed in their midst. But the intention of the section, as verses 9 *et seq.* particularly show, aims at diverting attention from his person and rôle, at destroying the opinion that he was concerned about the dogma of his school, and that they were concerned about discussing Paulinism, and the emphasis of verses 1-2 is placed not on the *I,* nor indeed on the *them,* but in the middle, between both, or rather above both, upon the gospel in which and by which "you have received." This "parelabete" must be understood here not only as an active verb, if it is (Lietzmann) to form no tautology to "I announced," but also solemnly: *This* reception (which subsequently recurs in verse 3) is, for the sake of its object, to be, from the outset, a binding one, an acceptance which compromises the recipient once for all and is irrevocable. It is not possible to do anything else here subsequently. Bengel interprets *Æternam hæc acceptatio obligationem involvit,* "This acceptance involves an eternal obligation."

To accept and afterwards release oneself, as if merely some tenets of Paulinism had been accepted, will not do. The Corinthians, however, *have* accepted: ye stand therein. The basis of their Christianity, the foundation of the Church, the "foundation" (iii. 10 *et seq.*), the steadfastness (xv. 58), is visible among them, whatever they may have built upon it, however uncertainly they may stand upon it. To falsify, deny, or forget this basis leads, indeed, to judgment, for if Christ be not risen, states verse 23 in extreme paradox, then our preaching is vain and your faith is vain also, i.e. verse 14: then this ground is for those who stand upon it not a basis, but an abyss. But where for me is an abyss, there is and abides the ground of God, and the lies and corruption which then intrude testify to the truth and the salvation which are there mocked. All these possibilities seem to Paul to alter nothing fundamentally with regard to the "acceptance," to alter in no wise the fact that what is involved is only "steadfast" and "unmovable." Of Christianity nothing too critical can be said—and Paul has in truth done so—of the power of the resurrection which stands behind Christianity, nothing too positive. Paul emphasizes: by which also ye are *saved*. Note the present tense, which makes the Greek words "Ye have received" and "stand" unequivocal. Their salvation is reality in the message, which they have received and in which they stand. Upon this most emphatic Yea the preceding criticism of Paul is based. We understand Paul aright if we feel this "ye are saved" as direct and unfounded. What then does Paul mean but this: the gospel whose messenger to you I was (from the standpoint of men) is in fact unmediated and unfounded, the divine Yea which is spoken to you, the last word of grace to each to whom it is said and by whom it is heard, the power of God unto salvation (Rom. i. 16). Luther commented upon this passage: "The world has it not and cannot do it, but the Word has it and can do it and it must therefore happen, for it is God's own strength and might. . . . It is really true that if feeling counted, I should be lost; but the Word is to rank over my and everybody's feelings and remain true, however insignificant it seems and however feebly it is believed by us. For all of us see and all of us experience the work that sins plainly damn us and condemn us to hell, that death consumes us and everybody, that no one can escape it; and you tell me of life and righteousness, of which I do not see a spark and which must be a weak life, to be sure. Yes, truly, a weak life for the sake of our faith. But, however weak it is, if only the Word and the spark remain in the heart, it shall become such a fire as shall fill life, heaven, and earth, and consume both death and disaster, like a drop of water, and so rend weak faith that no sin or death shall be seen or felt any more. But it needs a stronger struggle to retain the Word against our feeling and sight" (Erlangen Ed., li. 92-93). Obviously when Paul added this caution what he had in mind was not a restriction, but the acceptance of this "strong struggle." The sentence "in a certain word" is regarded by Lietzmann as a rhetorical question: "How have I preached it unto you, if ye keep it in memory?" I prefer to remain within the limits of the usual interpretation, and to regard the words "if ye keep in memory what I preached unto you" as a commentary upon the preceding "which," "wherein," and "by which" (in doing so Paul underlines the idea in the first sentence and emphasizes: *This* is what you have accepted, this is your ground, this saves you!) and the "if ye keep it" as indicating that the solemnly objective "receiving," "standing," "being saved," does not make the human Yes superfluous, but requires it. Luther speaks here directly of faith; Paul perhaps more soberly insists only upon a "keeping in memory," a retaining, not throwing away. Of course, he also means that "spark," the apex of the soul, in which the decision lies, not upon the reality of that which the gospel brings, but upon what is to be made of us by it. The second sentence carries the thought further: "unless ye have believed in vain." Now Paul is also speaking of belief. A belief can exist, large or small, strong or weak, which in itself is nugatory, vain, a belief in appearance. This must, however, mean here: a belief without object, without God. This belief does not hold fast to the accepted, fundamental, saving gospel, is worlds apart from the reality which it announces—nay, *brings;* nay, *is*. In verses 14 and 17 this menacing thought appears in reversed sequence. If the gospel is not true (as I brought it to you), then not only your preaching, but also your faith, is vain. But here, as there, the idea is to be understood as *argumentum ab absurdo*. Paul speaks of a possibility with which he neither intends nor is able to reckon. Judgment upon the Church, their faith being completely meaningless and without object, their being forsaken by God and the Holy Ghost—such things are impossible. The pronouncement in verse 34, "Some have not the knowledge of God," describes a border-line case. One can, one must, call him by this name, but only as such. But this is not quite what it means! The positive thing that Paul means here is just this: as surely as the belief of the Church, whether small or large, is not folly, but severity and truth, just as surely must it keep in memory the message declared unto it, the accepted, the fundamental, the saving message. Hence it can be reminded of this as of something which it already knows. Paul believes, not in the unbelief, but in the faith of the Corinthians. Thus the chapter stands from the outset under the sign of the hope of which it speaks.

"For I delivered unto you first of all that which I also received, how that Christ died for our sins according to the scriptures; and that He was buried, and that He rose again the third day according to the scriptures: and that He was seen of Cephas, then of the twelve: after that, He was seen of above five hundred brethren at once; of whom the greater part remain unto this present, but some are fallen asleep. After that, He was seen of James; then of all the apostles."—vs. 3-7.

The interest of the reader and the interpreter of this verse is usually concentrated upon one point, upon which, however interesting it might in fact be in itself, the interest of Paul was at any rate not directed. I am thinking, for instance, of Bousset's pages of exposition dealing with the relationship of this tradition of the resurrection of Jesus to the

Synoptic Gospels, and with the extraordinarily important question of the origin of the report of the
empty tomb, etc. As regards this, it must be emphasized that *neither* for Paul *nor* for the tradition, to
which we see him appealing here, was it a question
of giving a so-called "resurrection narrative," a
narrative of the historical fact "the resurrection of
Jesus," or even (Lietzmann) a "historical proof of
the resurrection." To *seek* things in this verse, such
as the oldest of the so-called "sources" of this fact,
or to *miss* such things as indications of localities and
times of the various appearances, or triumphantly
to record as *absent* such things as the mention of the
empty tomb—all this is really relevant only if we
persist in overlooking the object of this verse in the
context in which it stands, if we refuse to put, let
alone answer, the question whether all that Paul
meant here might not have the effect, not of dis-
connecting the *historical position of the question as
such,* but of *relativizing it.* Let us then for the time
being keep strictly to what Paul intended to say.
For I delivered unto you first of all that which I also
received. The purport of what was delivered and
received is described by the four sentences beginning with "that," to which four sentences all that
follows, up to and including verse 7, is to be sensibly
connected. A second thing that is delivered and
received does not follow, for what follows verse 8—
the appearance of the risen one to Paul himself—is
also part of what was delivered by him to the
Corinthians. It is not a second thing beside the
contents of verses 3-7, but an important confirma-
tion in this connexion of the contents of this verse.

"First of all" (verse 3) cannot therefore mean "in the first instance," as number one, but as the main point, as the central point, as the gospel plainly, and I regard it as allowable and incumbent to think of this "as the main thing" (first of all) in connexion with "which I also received." Paul's meaning is, "It was not, and is not, my idea to deliver to you the gospel in this perfectly definite outline which I preached unto you [verse 2], but I have so delivered it as I myself received it"—i.e. the gospel of the primitive Church has no other meaning than my gospel. It will profit you nothing to try to get behind Paul in order to procure a gospel that is alleged to be simpler and more acceptable, for if you go behind Paul you will stumble at the first step upon the same riddle that you think only Paul and Paulinism confronts you with now.

If we now consider the *contents* of verses 3 *et seq.*, what immediately strikes us is the verbal forms "he died, was buried, rose again, was seen." In the series of facts thus described, it is easy to establish the actual substance of that which Paul himself received and then delivered, and in doing so we should, at any rate, be in the presence of a so-called resurrection report, a narrative of events. But a closer consideration of the text immediately discloses, first of all, that the above-named four facts are by no means chronologically successive or in juxtaposition: the first, "he died," is characterized by the quite unhistorical addition "for our sins." The first and third, "he died" and "he rose again," by the addition "according to the scriptures," which in a historical proof, if that were the intention, would really be devoid of meaning. The fourth, lastly, "he was seen," extends fanshaped into a whole series of "was seen" as far as the "was seen" of Paul himself (verse 8), and is connected as a whole by "and" (not "then") with the preceding "he rose again," by no means merely to explain the latter, as would be the case if the point of the passage were a historical demonstration, but just rightly as Paul's own fourfold viewpoint at the end of the whole tradition. The most serious objection, however, to the "historical" interpretation is prompted above all by the third point, the "he rose again," if we compare it with verse 13: "If there be no resurrection of the dead, then is Christ not risen," sharply emphasized and repeated, and therefore certainly not to be understood in a merely rhetorical-dialectical sense (verses 15 and 16). The whole meaning of verses 12-28 is, indeed, this—that this historical fact, the resurrection of Jesus, stands and falls with the resurrection of the dead, generally. What kind of historical fact is that reality of which, or at any rate the perception of which, is bound up in the most express manner with the perception of a general truth, which by its nature cannot emerge in history, or, to speak more exactly, can only emerge on the confines of all history, on the confines of death? As little, at any rate, as this general truth is itself *fact*, for the reality of which the same man who wrote verses 12-19 will adduce *historical proof* in verses 3-7. As really chronological information only a phrase is left to us in verses 3-7, and that is the words "and was buried" in verse 4; but is it perchance possible from this sentence to understand historically the frontier of history looming before and behind, or would this be not the worst interpretation of the real facts: that rather *history*, which undoubtedly speaks in these words "and was buried," is here illuminated in the most dazzling manner, from the *frontier* of history, which is described by the words "who died" on the one hand, by the words "he rose again" on the other hand, while the words "he was seen" is the rendering of the many-voiced testimony (verse 15) that this boundary has been *seen.* In *history,* to be sure! But *in* history, the *frontier* of history, and indeed— and this is the vital point—not only from the *one* side, not only the "he died"—the death of Christ alone would not, in fact, be the frontier of history becoming visible; this fact alone would coincide with the second, the phrase "he was buried"—but also from the other side, that "God raised up Christ" (verse 15). This is in truth the *substance* of the testimony, and the origin of this testimony is just that fourfold "he was seen." This, then, is how the four facts are to be interpreted: not as a monotonous chronological recital of things of the same kind, but extremely graduated in a series several times interrupted: (1) Like two massive pillars: Christ *died* for our sins; and: Christ *rose again* on the third day; both being asserted, "according to the scriptures," as historical facts, to be sure, but, pray, *what kind* of historical facts? *This* end, the end of our sins, which yet can only end when history ends, and *this* beginning, the beginning of a new life, which yet can only begin when and where a new world begins.

(2) In the middle: "he was *buried,*" which is the unambiguous banal historical fact, but, and just

this, makes the case of Christ equally doubtful with
all human earthly things in general. Hope and fear,
belief and scepticism, are alike possible in face of
this tomb. This tomb may prove to be a definitely
closed *or* an open tomb; it is really a matter of
indifference. What avails the tomb, proved to be
this or that, at Jerusalem in the year A.D. 30?
"Christ died for our sins, Christ rose again on the
third day," Christ's end and beginning is *not* thereby
proved, and yet that is obviously what the tradition
delivered to the primitive Church, and Paul following it, meant to reveal as the main thing; but the
tomb, the demonstrable, stands in the midst like an
alpine hut in a deep valley between mountains
15,000 feet high, almost with a certain irony, one
might say, set there, if the matter were not so deadly
serious, in contrast to what on the left and on the
right is undemonstrable, nay is demonstrating itself,
is testified and is to be believed. And then confronting these two mountains and the valley between
is (3) a number of human eyes: Cephas, the Twelve,
five hundred brethren at once, all the apostles once
more. Time and place are a matter of perfect indifference. Of what these eyes see it can really be
equally well said that it was, is, and will be, never
and nowhere, as that it was, is, and will be, always
everywhere possible. As the expression of this state
of affairs there is no hint of an indication as to when
and where and by whom? As the expression of the
same state of affairs in the Synoptic and Johannine
reports, which profess, albeit differently from Paul,
to narrate (even they actually give no "resurrection report"): there is extreme obscurity and dis-

cordance in all indications of time and place and as
to the how? silence equally profound.   What do
these eyes see? we naturally feel impelled to inquire,
and to this question no other answer can be given
than: the tomb, the stone, the linen, the handker-
chief, and everything pertaining thereto; the evan-
gelical tradition, following its own point of view,
described in detail this residue and its discovery as
the *last* word that can be said on the basis of historical observation: a fact as doubtful as all earthly
facts are: he might, in fact, have been stolen, he
might only have appeared to be dead.   The Gospels
themselves do not make the least secret of the fact
that the sight of the empty tomb and the sight of the
risen Lord was something *toto cœlo* different, and it
is no glory for Christian theology that the idea
should even have occurred to it of engaging in
heated controversies in a critical or apologetic spirit
about this tomb, when it is as clear as noonday that
upon this subject, whatever may be thought from the
historical standpoint, the last word was said by the
authentic and priceless, in a double sense, concluding
words of the gospel of Mark xvi. 8: "for they were
afraid"; or, if a more positive utterance is preferred,
Luke xxiv. 5: "Why seek ye the living among the
dead?"   The human eyes of Peter, of the Twelve,
of the five hundred, etc., see just nothing but the
tomb and that the Lord is no longer there.   This
can mean everything.   Critically considered, it
might even mean: the tomb is the tomb, and he who
is dead does not return.   With more wisdom than
was subsequently shown, the Gospels themselves
drew no positive conclusions whatever from that

which was *thus* to be seen *there*. Paul in his way altogether refrains from saying what was to be seen there. The words "he was buried" say everything that is possible about the subject. He speaks, not of Cephas, the Twelve, the five hundred, and their "seeing," but of Christ, who *appeared* to (was seen by) them, and that must be understood by us as *two different things,* if we have only the least sensorium for the category of *revelation.* It is indeed somewhat strange to find in certain commentaries (we omit the names) the various "He appeared" of verses 5-7 carefully numbered (from 1 to 5), registered, collated with the Synoptic and Johannine narratives, and the one criticised and corrected with the aid of the others, in order to ascertain clearly what might have been "original" there! Of all that the New Testament says we need not, in fact, believe a single word, if we do not want to, but we must at least realize that it speaks of appearances of the *risen Christ;* we must at least grasp and respect this idea, and realize that what pertains to this idea, even if we cannot make anything of it ourselves, is not to be counted, weighed, and measured, as if it related to the conception of the historical Jesus, His closed or open tomb, which, in fact, the "sources" dispute with all their power. And, apart from everything else, may it not even be described as simple tactlessness out of the "He appeared," or what takes its place in the Gospels (of appearances of angels and subsequently of personal meetings with Jesus), to make, with the liberals, so-called visions (with the extraordinarily subtle distinction between "objective" and "subjective" visions), or, with the positivists, equally banal "historical facts," respecting which one can refer to the "sources" for support as in the case of all other facts, only with the distinction that what happens here is marvellous beyond comparison and that one is constantly exposed to the danger of running into the arms either of a Scylla of a gross mythology or the Charybdis of a coarse or refined spiritism?—quite apart from the bad historical conscience which we would develop, and which might suddenly drive us once more to the liberal friends of visions! As if this "positive" manner of asserting the resurrection of Jesus were not in fact the secret denial of the very thing which we would fain assert, the resurrection as the deed *of God*, whom no eye has seen nor ear heard, who has entered no human heart, neither outwardly nor inwardly, not subjective and not objective, not mystical nor spiritistic and not flatly objective, but as a historical divine fact, which as such is only to be grasped in the category of revelation and in none other.

"Appeared," said Paul of the third thing that happened there, in contrast to the historical "was buried," in contrast to the boundary marks "died" and "rose again." What does the Greek word mean? "He appeared, He rendered, He showed, He testified." But in all cases He. Even if we translate the word by "He was seen," it is still He. He who was laid in the tomb; but that does not now come into consideration. The tomb is doubtless empty, under every conceivable circumstance empty! "He is not here." To Christ's being in the tomb no further mention can be made. No, He who died for our sins and rose again on the third day, He, the crucified and risen Lord, *appeared*, the boundary of history and of mankind, the end and the beginning in one. All ideas as to the way in which this appearance was *seen* are incapable of being completed; they can only converge upon a denial of the appearance (whether we talk of visions or of external visibility) or else just lead back to the "seeing," which only has the tomb for its object. Only the appearance, that which He did, is, at any rate, the substance of the gospel, and, we can now very well say, the central substance of the gospel which Paul himself received and delivered, and to which it is his present intention to recall the Corinthians. For this appearance, by which, comprehensible only as revelation, or, in that case, not comprehensible at all, Jesus Christ as the end and the beginning, as the boundary and origin, as God's saving and life-giving Word, enters the horizon of this man: this appearance being only, in fact, the direct object of the Christian testimony (verse 15). *What* they testify is that Christ, who died for our sins, lives. What Paul wants to call the attention of the Corinthians to in verses 3-7 is that if they seek to push themselves behind or past him, Paul, back to the gospel of the primitive Church, they come up against the *same* testimony, the *same* "appeared" comprised in its whole incomprehensibility; that, however much they may turn and tack about, they must trip over this stumbling-block: Christ lives!—which, unless they overlook the witness of Christ generally—that is, desire to leave the Church—is in no way to be understood as a continuation of human experiences, and insights of a higher and the highest kind, but only as the witness of God's revelation, as the really genuine Easter gospel, within the very Church of Christ.

And, now that we have to some extent elucidated the meaning of these four facts, "died, buried, rose again, appeared," which form, so to speak, the skeleton of these five verses, we are in a position to clarify a number of not unimportant details in connexion with this reference to the gospel of the primitive Church. We refer to the words "according to the scriptures" of verses 3 and 4. It will be observed how the words "buried" and "rose again" are distinguished from the "buried" from which this addition is, probably wisely, omitted. What was intended to be the subject of historical proof would not need this addition, which would be necessary for that which presented itself as the subject of the testimony of revelation. That revelation is revelation can, of course, only be proved by revelation itself. The scriptural evidence is the preservation of *one* testimony of revelation by others, and to that extent the record of the harmony of revelation, in this case that testified by the prophets and by the apostles, in itself. The truth must prove itself, but in order to open our eyes to this, its self-proof, the concensus of voices, which announce the truth, is no insignificant matter. Paul knows that he is in harmony with the "scriptures" when, on the grounds of revelation, he testifies that Christ died for our sins and rose again on the third day. He sees the fathers of the Old Testament all standing around this one point in a wide circle, around this turning-point from death to life, from the end to the beginning, from an old to a new world, all gazing and pointing, knowing and participating, all expecting, believing, and promising in many different tongues nothing else than this *one*. All of them, with every historical limitation of human understanding, understand *that*. All of them, with all the historical obscurity which lies over their personalities and thoughts, are intelligible from this *point of view*. It cannot be a question of details. Just here, where plainly the Whole is involved, Paul certainly quotes no passages, and with good reason. He might, in fact, have done so—Isa. liii. 10-12, for example—but how much more eloquent is the effect of the solemn "according to the scriptures," which points like an outstretched arm to the Holy Narrative, than all quotation? In connexion with our passage this reference is, of course, bound to strengthen the impression, which Paul designs to create, that the Corinthians must not by any means think that the gospel, to which he is recalling them, is a fortuitous thing which might possibly be something different. The idea might in fact occur to them to go behind the primitive Church as well as Paul, to inquire of another suitable gospel. They must realize that, in that case, they would run into the arms of Job and the Psalmists, Jeremiah and Abraham, and that even there they have nothing better to expect than the one thing they would fain avoid. Observe, further, the "for our sins" in verse 3. I do not believe it is placed there merely for the sake of form. The hope of emancipation from sins was for the Corinthians, if this conclusion may be drawn from verses 17, 34,

56, a living and important idea, to which Paul might well be referring here. But his intention is to show them that this hope has stability only as *Easter* hope. What is the death of Christ to me if I am confronted with the "was buried"? Would it not be a sentimental illusion to glorify the *suffering* of Christ in itself, and to found one's faith upon the *sentiment* of Jesus which is therein preserved? Is the Crucifixion, with the bitter inquiry of God with which it ended, adapted for the foundation of a general religious truth that our sins are to be taken from us? Is not, for our absolution, a "And God spoke" necessary, and where is this to be found on Golgotha, or how could we hear it there, if we had not already heard it beyond all tombs as Easter gospel? If sins are a power, must not pardon then be a power, too, as universal—nay, even more universal, even more original, even more dominating than the former? If, however, sins rule, so long as time and as wide as the world are, what Word, then, is adequate to cope with sin as the last word of the victory which is not fought out in the world, not even in our hearts, nor even in our conscience, but *vanquishes* the world brought under one denominator? We might further ask: why the narrative of the appearances of the risen Lord, the "he was seen of Cephas, then the . . .?" That Paul was not concerned to name the greatest possible number of witnesses for the purpose of adducing the "historical proof" we have seen. Verses 5-7 have nothing whatever to do with supplying a historical proof and, thus, listening to the evidence of witnesses— not, however, for the reason that nobody in Corinth

had any need for a historical proof of the resurrection of Jesus, nor, again, for the reason that it was
not denied there at all (verses 12-18 are proof that
it was). What was disputed was the fundamental
radical application of the "resurrection of the dead,"
the treatment of *this* point of view as "the main
thing" (first *of all*) as Paul exercised it. For this
reason Paul fought, for his apostolic method, of
which he cannot even concede that it was perhaps
only *his* method, and for this reason he now conjures
up the cloud of witnesses, *not* to confirm the fact of
the resurrection of Jesus, not for that purpose at all,
but to confirm that the foundation of the Church,
so far as the eye can see, can be traced back to
nothing else than appearances of the risen Christ.
The Corinthians seem somehow to believe in the
miracle of the resurrection of Christ (perhaps they
believed with special enthusiasm in the empty
tomb!); but that the origin of Christianity along
the whole line is revelation, and only revelation,
they do not seem to have grasped, and now Paul
surrounds them, as it were, upon every side: Cephas,
the Twelve, more than five hundred, James, all the
apostles—wherever they may turn, everywhere this
"He appeared" flashes into their faces. Back!
back! everywhere bolted doors! Can the resurrection of the dead, he means to ask them, be denied in
the Church, which is in this sense founded on the
resurrection, as the most serious, the most actual
truth?

Certainly not by chance nor of secondary importance is inserted in its place the remarkable subordinate clause "of whom the greater part remain

unto this present, but some are fallen asleep." It
rebukes by anticipation the idea which is first
developed in verse 12 *et seq.*: the contrasts between
the resurrection of Jesus and that which was asserted
in Corinth as the last word about us: "We shall
fall asleep." Where people in Corinth saw something natural, for which a beautiful and edifying description was found, Paul perceives in the "falling
asleep" of Christians a problem (xi. 31). He cannot
acquiesce in the fact of dying. Neither the idea of
Providence, nor that of natural order, nor that of an
immortal soul, can appease him respecting the gulf
between death and life. The expression "the
nuisance of dying," which was uttered some years
ago, does not strike us as altogether un-Pauline.
Nothing to the contrary can be gathered even from
Phil. i. 21 *et seq.*, if the context be taken into account. Obviously what he means here is: How remarkable is the fact that men who have seen the
Lord have died! They saw the answer which the
death of Jesus found by God's power, and they did
not see the answer in their own death. Is this not
an intolerable relationship? If they have now only
"fallen asleep," despite the resurrection of Jesus, if
this is the last thing that is to be said about them,
and if the other five hundred and the other witnesses
named will also "fall asleep" when their time comes,
then the appearance of the risen Lord was for them
an experience like many others, one of the many experiences of so-called life, which is finally all over at
death. If this is so, Paul angrily concludes in verses
17-18, if the resurrection of Jesus were only an isolated miracle and not the revelation *of the* miracle

that God worked on men, if it is only to mean "Christ rose again" but not the "Resurrection of the Dead," then even this miracle is not true, then Christ is not risen, and those whom we now so amiably call "those that have fallen asleep" are perished (verse 18).   For then life and death are equally meaningless.

"And last of all He was seen of me also, as of one born out of due time.   For I am the least of the apostles, that am not meet to be called an apostle, because I persecuted the Church of God.   But by the grace of God I am what I am: and His grace which was bestowed upon me was not in vain; but I laboured more abundantly than they all; yet not I, but the grace of God which was with me. Therefore whether it were I or they, so we preach, and so ye believed."—vs. 8-11.

The verses complete what the preceding ones began, viz. the demonstration that the gospel which he, Paul, once brought to Corinth must inevitably and unalterably have the purport which it in fact has.   The difficulty which this knowledge encountered among the Corinthians has already been alluded to on several occasions: it consisted in the fact that in Corinth attention, which was detrimental to the cause, had been devoted, in part friendly, in part unfriendly, to his *person*.   It comes in effect to the same thing.   He was revered or opposed as something special, as the head of a school, as an apostle of his own kind, as Paul, and was thereby isolated, intentionally or unintentionally, from what he represented and said, from the cause which was really all that mattered.   Truth is mighty, however

modest may be its garb, as long as it has no name, no
tangible historical appearance, as long as we have
to do with it by itself. Truth is dead, or at least
mortally ill, as soon as it receives a human name,
or takes on human semblance, especially in the form
of a school, party, tendency or movement, which
carries a label, and is distinguished from like movements by definite slogans and customs. No better
method can be devised of keeping away from the
truth than to stamp it with this or that name, if
its own representatives themselves were not perhaps
so foolish as to do this. That is what Paul encountered in Corinth. In verses 3-7 he wrestled with
this object indirectly: "I say nothing that the
primitive Church did not also say." Now, he is
endeavouring to show directly to his readers the
difficult thing that he is, at any rate, he, Paul, and
not Peter, *not* James, that he, in fact, not only delivered that which he received from others, but that
he also received from first hand what he gave them,
in order, and at the same time, to divert them from
this false attention directed to his person and doc-
trines and, lastly and thirdly, at the same time, to show
them, with both these points, his own example, how
it is when the risen Lord appears to a man. "And
last of all he was seen of me also." As the last witness, but still as a witness, Paul also joins the ranks.
He cannot make the foundation of the Church anything but what it is, as it has in fact been laid; he
cannot go past it, because he himself was by its side.
Nor shall it be made a *reproach* to him that he has
only taken over a tradition from others and then
continued it. No, as surely as he also does this, just

as surely does he also know himself as a *source* of tradition, as an *originator*, not only as a continuer. If he is the last of whom this can be said, he must still emphasize that he is such an one. This will explain to the Corinthians why he strikes them as being repellent and alien. He, too, is just one of those of whom it is said: "he was seen of them." He must appeal to revelation. This is the burden that is laid upon him," woe to me if I do not preach the gospel" (ix. 16), this also gives him the right of going, consistently, his own road in their sight.

"As one born out of due time," an abortion beside the healthy children of the house, Paul feels, when he beholds himself the erstwhile persecutor of the Church of God, unworthy to be called an apostle! Why does Paul say all this, and just there? Certainly not out of a general desire to make himself out to be bad, and to humiliate himself, but assuredly in order now to demonstrate in his own person *ad oculos* what it means when the risen Lord appears to a man, in what kind of humiliation of the natural man this meeting finds expression, in what position a man then confronts God. Luther explains: "God does not want such cocksure and presumptuous spirits, but such people as have previously been through the mill, tempted and broken, and such must know and acknowledge that they have been sad knaves like St. Paul was and laden with such sins as spell right big sins for God, as enemies of God and the Lord Christ, so that they remain in humility and cannot presume or glorify themselves" (Erlangen Ed., li. 110). "By God's *grace* I am what I am." When everything has been said against him, Paul, that can be said, when nothing more is left of him, then that remains which really can remain, because it is from God. "By His *grace* I am . . . !" "The self-evidence of the truth was not in vain, my life was more laborious than that of others, I came in a thicker crowd, but all that is grace. Not I! I deserve and claim and am nothing. I live only by grace. But what I do by grace, that I *must* do, and I must be taken for what I am. Thus, no value attaches to any distinction between me and others. They, too, can only preach the risen Lord and the resurrection. Hear them or hear me! but hear! There is only one gospel, one faith, one salvation, one ground upon which we stand and ye with us."

§ 2

THE RESURRECTION AS THE MEANING OF FAITH
(*vs.* 12-34)

"Now if Christ be preached that He rose from the dead, how say some among you that there is no resurrection of the dead? But if there be no resurrection of the dead, then is Christ not risen: and if Christ be not risen, then is our preaching vain, and your faith is also vain. Yea, and we are found false witnesses of God; because we have testified of God that He raised up Christ: whom He raised not up, if so be that the dead rise not. For if the dead rise not, then is not Christ raised: and if Christ be not raised, your faith is vain; ye are yet in your sins. Then they also which are fallen asleep in Christ are perished. If in this life only we have hope in Christ, we are of all men most miserable."—vs. 12-19.

The purpose of the section verses 12-34 is to remove from under the feet of the Corinthian Christians the ground upon which they have placed themselves, and to set them upon the ground of revelation, of divine truth, and reality, to which the two following sections, verses 35-49 and verses 50-58, refer. It is a repugnant work of destruction in its way that is carried out here; at any rate, a remarkable contribution to the chapter: Paul and his Church. Paul does not shrink from putting his "Either-Or" so sharply that beside the impossible, unbelievable, inaccessible gospel of the Resurrection of the Dead there is left only the abyss of an utterly radical scepticism towards everything divine, even towards everything that is humanly highest, holding the danger that somebody may fall into it and be unable to get out. At this point we must recall Pascal and Kierkegaard, and the fundamental distinction between a prophet and a churchman generally. The Church seeks how it may come to terms with this ultimatum. Of the needs of a Church composed of believers, half believers, and unbelievers no account is taken here at all. The viewpoint of education seems to be completely excluded. The possibility, for example, that one could emerge from an imperfect faith, gradually develop to a perfect one, from a Christianity *without,* to a Christianity *with,* the resurrection of the dead is not taken into consideration. The last word, verse 34, is as irreconcilably sharp as the first, verse 12. *If* anyone could feel themselves understood, justified, and strengthened here, it would be the secretly wholly unbelieving, as in the Synoptic Gospels. At bottom, of course, not even they, but in no case the believing, who here at first only hear a No. It is quite distinct here: the apostle is not conducting the business of

Corinthian Christianity, but he is the witness of his Lord, and they are to make of it what they will. As witness, not as pastor in our sense, he builds the Church. The section is clear, provided we bear in mind that verses 20-28 are a long digression. Here he is speaking of the *real* meaning of the Christian faith; in verses 29-34, he returns once more to the negative line, which he had left in verse 19, to the demonstration that every *other* alleged meaning of Christian faith was nonsense.

Let us turn to details. Verse 12 proceeds upon the assumption that the substance of the preaching of Christ is that He rose from the dead. It was that, indeed, which Paul aimed at showing in verses 1-11. Run to Peter, run to James, run to whichever of the many hundreds of the first Churches you like, every where you will find, at the beginning of their testimony, that "appeared," the act of God on the verge of history, which opens a new eternal history, the Crucified as the Lord of Life and Death. From verse 12 onwards, Paul assumes that this is conceded to him, albeit in its whole bearings it is not understood. The belief in the resurrection of Christ, which Paul did not need to prove to the Corinthians, because they were at least supposed to affirm it, inasmuch as it was not excessively difficult to affirm it as a remote miracle, this belief has no *fundamental* and no vital significance for them. It must, in any case, be missing. It is a *fragment,* but not the *whole.* They are not thinking from this standpoint. At this point Paul intervenes. How can the resurrection of the dead be denied, if the substance of the gospel of Christ, which they believe, is *this,* that Christ rose from the dead? Luther was right enough when he said that to proceed as Paul proceeded here was a weak *dialectica* or demonstration among heathen and unbelievers, that is *probare negatum per negatum* ("to prove a negative by a negative"), or *petere principium* ("to beg the principle"), and the meaning of Paul's whole proof may be summarized in the sentence: God is God (*op. cit.*, 120 f.). In fact, the conclusion from Christ to us others is based upon the far deeper-lying assumption that the resurrection of Christ, in that "appeared," to which Paul appealed in the name of the primitive Church and in His own name, was a question of the revelation of God. If that be true, if the end of history set by God is here, if the new eternal beginning placed by God appears here, then that which has appeared from God applies to the whole of history within the scope of this horizon, then the miracle of God to Christ is immediately and simultaneously the miracle of God *to us*, and not a miracle about which it may, at any rate, still be asked: What has it to do with us? If we see God at work there, then what is true there is also serious for us here and now, then our life, too, it goes without saying, is placed in the light which proceeds from that horizon of all that we call life. Not yet in fulfilment. We are, indeed, still living this life, as yet, we, indeed, only know time; it is the "not yet" which separates us from the resurrection. But we are living the life limited by that horizon, we are living in time for eternity, we are living in the hope of the resurrection, it is that which cannot be denied, if Christ's resurrection is to be understood, not as miracle or myth or psychic experience (which all come to the same thing), but as God's revelation.   For it just means in fact: "God is God, Either-Or, yes or no, but not: He is God there, but not here in Corinth, but not for us." Christ is risen, but we know and are living only this unending, horizonless life, lacking a last promise. This second and decisive assumption: Christ is not only risen in the same sense as Julius Cæsar was murdered, and the battle in the Teutoburger wood was fought, but in the sense that God has spoken and acted here; this second assumption is, at any rate for the Corinthians, a *negatum; this* range of the historical truth believed by them they just do not grasp, and to that extent Paul proves to them the truth of the other *negatum,* the resurrection of the dead, actually *per negatum,* by that first which they have not comprehended.   The artifice of this section is that Paul, from the outset, imparts to what is admitted by the Corinthians a meaning which is as strange to them as that which is not admitted by them, the general resurrection of the dead, and hence takes them by surprise and disconcerts them.   And Luther was perfectly right when he said: "Thus this text disputes powerfully and is the right way to defend our doctrine, for we cannot prove our faith and all the articles in any other manner" (*op. cit.,* p. 123), except that with Paul the whole matter is without the apologetic tendency which, remarkably enough, appears in Luther's exposition.   That is to say, Paul actually does not now prove *negatum per negatum,* but he refutes just the *concessum per negatum.*   He shows the Corinthians that if the general resurrection of the dead is of no significance, then neither the historical resurrection of Christ nor a number of other alleged truths believed by them is of any significance. He does not defend himself, but he attacks: Christianity without resurrection, and says as forcibly as he can, that it is a lie and a deceit, not because it is still without this article of faith, but because it is in itself an illusion, a fiction. Whereas they regard Paul as a dogmatist, who loads their reason with an unnecessary, unrealizable idea, he shows them that they are those who (not with their doubts and negations, but with what they admit and presumably also *believe*) are playing blind-man's-buff with ideas divorced from the real actuality. In attempting to escape from the resurrection as the alleged absurd, they are making an absurdity of what to them appears *not* absurd, but reasonable and tolerable; they are sawing off the branch upon which they are sitting.

"But if there be no resurrection of the dead, then is Christ not risen" (verse 13). If it be that we men are simply drops of water in the infinite, horizonless sea of life, if there are no Last Things, no crisis, which puts this whole in question and at the same time supplies the answer, rises up like a minus in front of the bracket and at the same time places under a new positive sign—if life and death are to be conceived as natural events within this great general endless life that we know, events beside or behind which there may also be yet others, but also *within* the same one whole—then, says Paul, I would go but one short step farther, and say: Christ, *too*, is not risen. If my life and all our lives do not stand in the light of that divine horizon, then I must accordingly interpret otherwise my beginning in Christ and, consequently, that of the primitive Church: then the divine horizon of all things has by no means appeared there, then that which happened there may be interpreted as a miracle, myth, or inward experience, in this way or that; it then belongs, in any case, to the sea of life, among the many shapes and events, which may be explained in this way or that. "Christ is risen" then means, fundamentally, as much and as little as "Christ is not risen." What is referred to even there cannot be anything that is qualitatively new and different. If God is not God in *our* life, then He is also not that in the life of *Christ*. How do we manage at all to recognize, let alone affirm, something there that we do not know and assert for ourselves? Why, for pious and dogmatic reasons, hold fast to something that has no significance? If no dead are to arise except the One, then the resurrection of even this One is an offence dispensable, unimportant, a foreign dualistic element in a philosophy otherwise uniform, and regarding which it is only a question of religious tactics whether we amiably lend it a poetic interpretation or bluntly deny it. Either God is known and recognized as the Lord and Creator and Origin, because He has revealed Himself as such, or there is no revelation in history, no miracle, no special category "Christ." If the latter be the case, "if Christ be not risen (verse 14) then *is* our preaching vain, and your faith *is* also vain." The answer to the foregoing might, indeed, run that the abolition of the special category Christ, the idea of a revelation history, is,

in fact, a possibility. What is the position then?
The Christian gospel, then, still resounds: Christ
the Messiah of God. But how does it stand with the
severity and weight of this assertion?   Is it more
than an assertion?   Does it become more illuminating by ascribing to the Messiah the attributes
Hero, Prophet, Witness, the complete attributes of
personal life?   Does it not become even more questionable when it is condensed into the assertion that
He is the Son of God?   How do we contrive to say
such things, to decorate Jesus with such superla-
tives? What do all the others say, at the most, but:
we *fancy*, we *wish*, we *believe*, we *know* Him, but
this way will never lead to an unequivocal: *He* is.
This unequivocal *He is*, which would make Christian preaching alone, preaching as distinct from mere
protestation, which must be its proper substance,
would then necessarily, however skilfully the doctrine may be draped, be *missing*. In that case, it
may be brought to a "doctrinal faith," but no longer
as a *kerygma*, "proclamation"; for *kerygma* is based
on revelation, and revelation is in fact denied.
Christ is not risen, but, however one regards His
resurrection, even as only a particle of the general
life (however perfect or exemplary a life it might be)
this is no category *for itself*. The last word that in a
strictly realistic manner can be said of Him, must,
in fact, be no more than this, that He was a man,
and, as such, died. Even *His* light cannot triumph
over the obscurity in which this life known to us is
wrapped. In other words: the *preaching* is vain, and
the faith that is founded by it is vain. Both may
nevertheless be intimate, upright, and inspired, they

will only lack just the specific gravity of the divine object, which can only be *preached,* which can only be *believed.* Even the faith, without reference to revelation, will be a substitute faith, not addressed to God, but to the human something in Christ, whose divine resemblance is there asserted. In that case, Christianity has, for preacher and hearer, quite smoothly slid back into the catalogue of religions, of which the human value is certainly not to be under-estimated, but which can in no way claim to be and remain something more than human. This empty shell may be beautifully painted with some gold leaf and create an edifying impression, but somewhere in the centre dwells the despair of the sincerity which realizes that Jesus has in fact died, and that a dead Messiah, whatever beautiful things may be said of Him, cannot be the *Messiah.* Life goes on its way, time hurries, history is endless, as if no Jesus had been. If it be so, Paul continues, if revelation be no plain truth of *life,* then it is also no historical truth, then we apostles are false witnesses of God. In that case, our place is in the long line of churchmen, who for the weal or consolation of mankind, and under the imminent suspicion of serving ourselves more than God, claim an authority which nobody has given us—theological auguries and auspices, who cannot meet without significantly smiling at each other, in the consciousness of the fatal secret of the utter insignificance of their activity. Of parsons it can simply be said that they talk of things which they understand no more than anybody else. We stand, then, in the shadow of the curse which lies over all religions. Religion appears with the claim,

with the dignity of revelation. What becomes of it
when it *openly* renounces such claim?   But what
becomes of it when it *secretly* renounces such claim,
when it has not the courage to believe in revelation?
Then, Feuerbach is right. Then, it is to be explained
as no more than the dream of human wishes. Then,
it is time to divest it of its dignity, and to address it
as it in truth is. The gospel of a risen Christ, so far
as it is not fundamentally preached and accepted as
God's word for all time, is flatly a rebellion against
the truth of *God*. For the truth of God for all times,
and for the whole world (apart from His revelation),
does not mean that it gives itself a religious inner-
worldly redemption, as the auguries maintain, but
that *judgment* and *perishing* rule there.

And so it is with Christianity, says Paul, if Christ
be not risen. "For if the dead rise not, then is not
Christ raised" (v. 16). And, then, once more, your
faith is vain (v. 17). The Christian faith does not
live of itself, but by its relation to the faithfulness of
God. If this is withdrawn—and the denial of the
resurrection, Christian monism, means that it is
withdrawn, that the relation to God becomes the
relation to the unending—then the faith falls back
upon itself. No one will dispute that, even so, it has
its importance as the expression of deprivation and
of longing, but not otherwise, not as a certain "confidence." It cannot avoid being compared to the
man who tried to pull himself out of the mire by
his own boot laces, and in no case can it escape being
compared with other religions. The Corinthians are
of opinion that in their "religion" they have something incomparable. We sometimes speak of an

"absoluteness of *Christianity*." That expression, at any rate, has no meaning if Christ is not risen, if He is not a category for Himself. In that case, Christianity is very relative. And this means in a practical sense: "you are still in your sins." Sin is too serious a matter to be overcome by religious protestations and enthusiasms. It is a dominion over man, not merely a moral defect that attaches to him. It is given with his existence as a child of Adam, and is only to be overcome with his existence. On the other hand, the word *forgiveness* of sins is also a serious word, a sovereign, deliberate act of God's rule stands behind, a new world breaks in, where forgiveness is preached and believed. Sins *consoled* are not sins *forgiven,* and a forgetting and passing over of sins in the abundance of religious feeling still less so. There is no *inner* worldly overcoming of sins. If Christian truth is only *inner* worldly, if it is not the *end* of all things, you are still in your sins, and to preach and believe the contrary is a sentimentality, an illusion of illusions, which sooner or later will bitterly avenge itself upon those who suppose they are converted and born again. And to the same category, then (verse 18), belongs that which we are accustomed to say about those that are asleep in Christ, about the blessed continuance of life in the beyond, about that in Kingdom Come. A poor saviour for the living will hardly be a better one for the dead. If the world and the life that we know is endless, then the belief in the beyond is also only an expression in idealism, with which we affirm the endless progress of this man; then what applies to the remoter spheres, unknown to the majority of men, of the life beyond, and to the stages and stations which man may reach there, may also be said of his life this side of death: judgment and destruction also rule there. Or whence comes the desire to know anything else? Whence do we lay claim to the arrogance that dying means redemption? Dying is pitilessly nothing but dying, only the expression of the corruptibility of all finite things, if there be no *end* of the finite, no *perishing* of the corruptible, no *death* of death. We are not, with edifying enthusiasm, to just try and push past the fact of death, but to be right sober at the last (verse 34), just as in front of the Cross of Christ, and say to ourselves, that this last word attainable by us: that we must *die,* gives, at any rate, no occasion for religious optimism regarding our situation as understood apart from revelation.

Verse 19 summarizes the result so far: If, in this life only, we have hope in Christ, we are of all men most miserable. Bousset comments on this verse as follows: "In conclusion, Paul even proceeds to an assertion which we cannot approve and follow. We are rather of opinion, however firmly we hold with Paul the hope of eternal life, that, even if there should be no hope of eternal life, a life faithful to the spirit of Jesus and spent in sacrifice would stand higher and be even happier than a life passed in undisturbed sensuality!" A remarkable misconception of the position! As if eternal life and the life beyond were the same thing with Paul! And as if the hope of eternal life would have been something so limited for Paul, unless he happened to be over-excited, that he would need to be subsequently slapped on the shoulder, to call his attention to the fact that things were not so bad after all, and that a really Christian life, even without this hope, was at least a feasible proposition! No, in this verse, and again in the concluding verses of the section, verses 29-34, is shown just the invincible common sense of Paul, who, on the one hand, in speaking of *this* life, has also drawn the so-called life *beyond,* according to verse 18, into the life for which, according to the theory of the Corinthians, there is *no* redemption, and who, on the other hand, by what he calls "hope in Christ only in this life," understands something far more radical than modern shortness of breath. One need only experimentally translate the ϵἰ, "if," by "so far" and provisionally ignore the word "only" in order to see immediately what Paul means. In this life in all seriousness to hope in Christ is, for Paul, actually something fearful in itself. If this hope be taken seriously, it puts a man in a perfectly impossible situation. In doing so he places himself, in fact, under the judgment which, notoriously, begins in the House of God among his own people. There it is perceived that man is under the dominion of sin, there the fragility of all temporal things is perceived. There the problem of existence as such is felt. There man becomes homeless and troubled, inwardly and outwardly. There one stands under the Cross. What then do the others know of it, who do *not* hope in Christ? Christ does not make life intolerable to them, does not make of it a great question. They have enough hiding-places to get into a place of safety. To Christians they are closed.

"They bear anxiety and woe in their hearts at God's anger, and the fear of eternal death, which will make them companions of the Devil in the abyss of Hell, lies on them day and night; they must fight so that they might sweat bloody sweat: that I would rather lie a year in prison and suffer hunger and thirst than suffer a day of such hellish torture from the Devil, with which he attacks the Christians who yet believe. . . . For they all have here the two ways in front of them and the Devil and their own conscience against them, which tells me that they are not pious . . . that there is no more wretched being living on earth than a Christian . . . of this the other great multitude know nothing whatever . . . are confident and joyful, experience nothing of such heart-anguish." (Not Calvin but Luther, Erlangen Ed., li., pp. 132-135.)

This Christian life then, this hope in Christ, limited to life, conceived without the divine horizon, without the certainty of resurrection—what else would this be than perfect nonsense, the most terrible and double self-deception? The happiness of children of this world eludes the Christian: why are they not themselves children of this world, why are they not happy here and now, if promise and fulfilment may yet be sought and found within the world? Instead, they delude themselves as *Christian* children of the world with a hope that cannot be fulfilled and to which the others, wiser than they, rightly do not surrender themselves. What meaning can their privation and their hope have, unless it refers to the crisis from life to death to life, to the life of the resurrection, unless therefore they hope in Christ not in this life *alone* but radically beyond this life? The idea of verse 19 is therefore not eudæmonist: out of the difficulty and distress of the Christian life springs the postulate of a compensation beyond, and therefore a resurrection, but here also critically: the absence of the hope of resurrection, like the resurrection of Christ (v. 13), like the *kerygma* and the faith (verse 14), like the forgiveness of sins (verse 17), and the faith in beyond (verse 18), renders the Christian existence with its paradoxy as a whole (verse 19) a farce, a folly, and an absurdity. The meaning of a Christianity without resurrection, this remarkable assertion, faith, confession, hope, and struggle, the meaning of this in affirmation and negation, in action, speech, and experience, in outward and inward appearance an equally extravagant situation, is nonsense itself, if the resurrection of the dead is not the very central point to which all this relates, if God is not just God. But now Paul breaks off; he will once more revert in verse 29 to this icy train of thought which threatens to shake Christianity to its foundations. For the moment he continues as follows:

"But now is Christ risen from the dead, and become the firstfruits of them that slept. For since by man came death, by man came also the resurrection of the dead. For as in Adam all die, even so in Christ shall all be made alive. But every man in his own order: Christ the first-fruits; afterwards they that are Christ's. [Full stop after αὐτοῦ.] *At His coming, then cometh the end* [in this last period] εἶτα [is not third member to ἀπαρχή and ἔπειτα, verse 23, but closer definition to εν τῇ παρουσίᾳ; τὸ τέλος does not mean "the rest," and not even the "end," but

adverbially, like 1 Pet. iii. 8, "finally"], when He shall have delivered up the Kingdom to God, even the Father; when He shall have put down all [his own] rule and all authority and power [here dash instead of full stop]*⸺ for He must reign, till He hath put all His enemies under His feet*—[dash instead of full stop] *the last enemy that shall be destroyed is death, for [it is written]: He hath put all things under His feet. But when He [Christ] saith: all things are put under Him!* [dash instead of comma]*—it is manifest that He is expected, which did put all things under Him*—[dash instead of full stop] *and when all things shall be subdued unto Him, then shall the Son also Himself be subject unto Him that put all things under Him, that God may be all in all."*—vs. 20-28.

I would observe that in the characteristic features of the exegesis of this complicated passage already given in this translation I have followed Hofmann, who in turn follows Zündel. Its weakest point is, probably—to admit this openly at once—the meaning of εἶτα "then"—Luther translates *darnach* (afterwards)—in verse 24. I admit that its comprehension as third member to "firstfruit" and "then" seems obvious at first glance. But if "the end" be translated "the remainder" (Leitzmann), we are faced with the fact that in what follows no further mention is made of the resurrection of this remainder. If we translate it by "the end" (Weizsäcker, Bousset), it is not easy to see how "the end" as the third member is to fit in with Christ as the first and his own as the second member. The difficulty of Hofmann's interpretation of εἶτα "then" seems to me a lesser and more acceptable difficulty in comparison. The acceptance of the sentences in verses 25 and 27 placed in dashes or brackets seems to me to go without saying. In any case, we have to do with a peculiarly contorted, extravagant construction of thought and sentence, and, once we have grown accustomed to Hofmann's arrangement of sentences, which, in my opinion, moreover, assorts quite well with the Pauline genius for speech, it will be found to throw a flood of light upon the whole. In verse 28, note that "the" before αὐτός is to be underlined. We understand the passage wrongly if we think that what Paul meant here was also that of the Son, whereas he means: The Kingdom of the Son has then reached its end. Opinions may differ regarding the relation of the end of the sentence with ἵνα, with that in verse 28 to ὑποτάξαντι, that to which all is subject, instead of to ὑποταγήσεται, he will subdue himself, as is usually done. But in any case it imparts to it more meaning and greater compactness to the whole than the usual interpretation. Hofmann's exegesis as a whole has convinced me because its result signifies a great *simplification*. If it is correct, then Paul had developed here no eschatological mythology, but in impetuous crowding metaphorical language expresses the following clear ideas: Christ as the second Adam is the beginning of the resurrection of the dead. Perfection is the resurrection also of His own, and therefore the very fundamental thing that was denied in Corinth. This perfection is, as the abolition of death generally, His highest and at the same time His last act of sovereignty. As yet He is not fulfilled (*vollzogen*), His power is still in conflict with the other penultimate powers, and to that extent we are now standing in

His Kingdom, awaiting that last, but only just *awaiting.* When He is fulfilled, then His Kingdom, as a special Kingdom *beside* the Kingdom of God (His Kingdom as the period of the merely "adjacent" Kingdom of God, the period of hope, which is indeed hope but no more than *Hope*), is at an end. To this end has the Kingdom in fact been given him, that God should be all in all. Therefore this "God all in all," and hence the general resurrection of the dead, is the meaning, misconceived in Corinth, of the resurrection of Christ, the meaning of the Christian faith.

Let us consider a few details. With the words "but now is" (verse 20) Paul turns away with an energetic jerk from the situation, perceived to be untenable, which must arise from the ignoring of the revelation, to the latter itself. If God is God, then the position is not, as is assumed in verses 12-19, that the godlessness, spiritlessness, and disconsolate state of the human situation give the lie to the resurrection of Jesus and Christianity, but that, on the contrary, the resurrection is the solution, the light of hope which falls on this situation. The metaphor of the firstfruits derives from the Old Testament. "God claimed *this* portion of the harvest for Himself and thereby gave to understand that the other part, the whole, belongs to Him." That is our hope; the meaning of the resurrection of Jesus consists in this, that the resurrection is the divine horizon also of our existence. Life and the world are finite. God is the end. Hence He is also the beginning. Now there is a meaning when we speak of the dead as "fallen asleep." The position then is (if the Corinthian *negatum* that God is God is *no* longer *negatum*) "that the resurrection is to be so regarded and understood as if it had already affected Christ; in fact, already more than half already happened; that what still exists of death is to be regarded as nothing but a deep sleep and the future resurrection of our body is to occur no differently than from being suddenly awakened from such sleep" (Luther, *op. cit.* p. 140). Behind the impenetrable walls of impenetrable reality in front of which we stand, and whose unmistakable sign is death, stands and awaits the new real life, which has appeared in Christ, but is the very life of all of us. Contrasted with each other (verses 21-22)—and that is the universal which the Corinthians, in their religious position that is alien from reality, are unable to see—are the old and the new man: Adam, with whom death, Christ, with whom life, begins. With the decision upon this antithesis of heaven and earth is bound up the decision upon the truth or falsehood of that which Christians think they believe and possess. Thence comes light, but thence also come shadows. "In Adam all die," is the account of every human life ruled off; "in Christ shall all be made alive." Note the antithesis of present and future. The former indicates our condition with which we have to reckon; the latter is the promise in which we may hope. Observe, also, the "all," obvious from the start, the later following "who belong to Christ" (Christ's), to be understood, not as exclusive, but as representative. The resurrection, like death, concerns *all*. But it is to be borne in mind (verse 23) that the last word, the executed decision between Christ and Adam, comes, for us, within the category of a "not yet." Each in his place (in the order of God). Another is Christ; another are we. To know the revelation of God in Christ means to place oneself within its promise, not proleptically in a supposed *fulfilment*. The projecting "afterward" reminds one of Col. iii. 1 *et seq*: "Our life is hid with Christ in God." Not in vain is Calvin's exegesis more vigorous at this passage than elsewhere. What obtrudes here is his special idea of Christ. But it remains neither with the concealment of Christ nor with that of our life, and consequently in no case with resignation. Waiting means really *looking towards* something that is just coming, and here it is only Paul's intention to testify vigorously to this coming as such. It is the arrival, nay, the presence, of the hidden Christ and His victory, with which the resurrection even of His own is occurrence. Christ's *parusia* is nothing different, second next to His resurrection, only the definite coming-to-the-surface of the same subterranean stream which in revelation for the first time became perceptible in time, the *fulfilment* of that which in time can only be grasped as a *promise*. In order to understand, we must here, as in the case of the resurrection, try to form the idea of a *boundary* of all time, except that it is now not merely revealed and believed, but —and with this our idea of time loses all intelligibility—finally *marked*, the "God is God" without any dialectical tension as *given*. "God is all in all," as it runs lastly. This is the general victory of Christ announced in the resurrection, which, once known in its absoluteness, although never and nowhere

present, is yet always and everywhere to be conceived of as the crisis of every human temporal
thing.   It is that which Paul has practically confirmed as an apostle, and here he is not at one with
the Corinthians.

Observe now how the idea of the outlook upon
this last is developed in the following. From verse
24 onwards Paul emphasizes, through all the inter-
ruptions which he permits himself, the present state
of the world, but also our present relationship to
God, even the Christian one, is a provisional state,
an episode, an episode indeed of the transition and
the struggle. In this sense we are now standing in
the Kingdom of Christ in the relationship of revelation and faith "wherein God reigns through the
Word, not in the visible public being, but like as the
sun is seen through a cloud. There we see the light,
but the sun itself we do not see, but when the clouds
roll away we see both, sun and light, at the same time
in one being" (Luther, *op. cit.*, pp. 159 f.).

The error of the Corinthians may be understood
in this wise: they comprehended what had happened in Christ in the world as something finished
and satisfying in itself. In reality it is only a beginning, in fact only an indication; Christ is come
to deliver the Kingdom to the Father, after He has
taken their force away from the powers warring
against God, and has undermined the world, so to
speak (Zündel) (verse 24). The hostile powers are
all independent beginnings and forces, whose relationship to God is not yet clear. We must see Christ
in *conflict* with all that is in this sense obscure, not
at peace with it. The Christian monism of the

Corinthians, who regarded the Kingdom of God as already established, is a pious godlessness. No, the Kingdom of God is in course of coming, and *that* is characteristic for our situation in Christ. His sovereignty, the exercise of His power in the name of God, is in full *swing*, and no appeasement, no satisfaction with an existing Christian state, is possible there (verse 25). As Christ Himself allows His enemies no peace, so for Christians there can be no security of an alleged possession in the shadow of the coming; how can it when their Lord is even in the field? The aim of the movement, which is the meaning of the Kingdom of Christ, is the abolition of death (verse 26). Death is the peak of all that is contrary to God in the world, the last *enemy*, thus not the natural lot of man, not an unalterable divine dispensation (cf. verse 6 and xi. 30). Peace cannot and must not be concluded just here in such a way as to establish a spiritual-religious-moral Kingdom of God on earth, the while forgetting the *enemy*. There is peace only in prospect of the *overcoming* of the *enemy*. What makes Paul angry with the Corinthians is that in the hope established in the resurrection of Jesus they have forgotten and betrayed His comprehensive and interpenetrating ruler's power; that, among them, blind Nature, or fate, stands between God and men as an indissoluble knot, with which one somehow compounds (religiously, if possible), whereas he sees the Lord striding from *struggle* to *struggle* and finally approaching the inconceivable supreme *victory*. The Kingdom of Christ—that is, the Kingdom of transition and of struggle—cannot be at an end so long

as God has not yet subdued *all* things to it (verses
26-27). What is said about men generally in Ps.
viii., 7, Paul applies here to Christ. The cry of
Christ, "All things are put under His feet" (verse
27) (in this connexion we may be permitted to think
of the Johannine "It is finished," John xix., 30, as
the *counterpart*), described the goal attained and the
end of *His* Kingdom. The parenthesis "it is manifest," once more describes this Kingdom expressly
as an *episode;* the Messianic Kingdom is not eternal.
Beyond the militant and triumphing Christ is always
God Himself. Because *God* reigns and designs to
reign in Christ, Christianity is a serious affair; *that*
is the meaning of faith. But if that call can sound,
if it be true that all things are under His feet, that
all relative things are as such abolished, then the
reign of Christ is at its goal, then the Kingdom of
God has dawned, which is the meaning of the Kingdom of Christ. Thus God stands now where this
Last Thing is not yet, in a *not yet* definitely ordered
relationship to the world. That God is all in all,
is not true, but must *become* true. Christian monism
is not a knowledge that is presently possible, but a
coming knowledge. If it is to be genuine, it must
only be comprehended now as Christian dualism,
as the tension between promise and fulfilment, between "not yet" and "one day," and it may *not* be
anticipated. To set right what is in disorder, to
abolish what is provisional, to overcome dualism,
to bring about the "God who is all in all," *such* is
the mission and significance of Christ. To expect
all things from Him, therefore—but, be it thoroughly

understood, to *expect* all things from Him—is the meaning of faith.

> *"Else what shall they do which are baptized for the dead, if the dead rise not at all? Why are they then baptized for the dead? And why stand we in jeopardy every hour? I protest by your rejoicing which I have in Christ Jesus our Lord, I die daily. If after the manner of men I have fought with beasts at Ephesus, what advantageth it me, if the dead rise not? let us eat and drink; for to-morrow we die. Be not deceived: evil communications corrupt good manners. Awake to righteousness, and sin not; for some have not the knowledge of God: I speak this to your shame."*—vs. 29-34.

In the digression verses 20-28 Paul positively expounded the meaning of the Christian faith, the Kingdom of Christ, the second Adam. But as the first Adam brought death, so the second brought life, the resurrection. In other words: as the resurrection is obviously not yet here, the Kingdom of God is not yet finished, not even in what the Christian Church has and is in its faith. The meaning of the Kingdom of Christ, and therefore also the meaning of the Christian faith, is never exhausted in that which is present and given. It is rather in its essence a hope and expectation of what at all times is only coming, only promised, the Kingdom of God, of the Father, in which there are no longer any princedoms, powers, and authorities, no greatness and splendour that would be secondary to the grandeur and splendour of God, in which therefore also the last enemy, death, is thus abolished. Christians

must grasp the idea that the last word of the Kingdom of Christ is its end in the *Kingdom* of *God*, the
last word of faith is its end in *fulfilment*. The *Kingdom* of *God*, or *fulfilment*, is not, as may so easily
be thought, a higher continuation of this life, but just
the resurrection of the dead. Faith, i.e., to be in the
Kingdom of Christ, means to await the *resurrection*.

But, as I have already said, the tendency of the
whole section of verses 12-34 is critically negative.
Hence Paul now returns, verse 29, to the line which
he had left, where the issue was the destructive effect
of the demonstration: a Christianity which has not
this meaning of the Kingdom of *Christ*, i.e. of the
Kingdom of *God*, i.e. the *abolition* of *death*—such a
Christianity is nonsense. Here he again resumes
the argument and proceeds to a conclusion. Verse 29
is a *crux interpretum*, and the reader must make up
his mind that even I cannot tell him much that is
satisfying on this point. What is the meaning of
"which are baptized for the dead"? To be really
baptized again for others who are already dead, to
be baptized vicariously for them? He can himself
read in Calvin with what indignation the latter protests against the assumption that Paul could have
employed here such an obviously superstitious custom as a means of proving a thing, without saying a
word against this scandal. But Luther also announces with an emphatic "That is nothing" his
reluctance to accept this interpretation. Similarly,
among the moderns, Bengel and Hofmann. I should
like nothing better than to join such good company.
But what are we to make of it when Luther for his
part explains: "They had themselves baptized

among the graves of the dead as a sign that they
certainly believed that the dead who lie thus buried
and over which they were baptized would rise again"
(*op. cit.*, li. 191).

Can "for the dead" mean "among the graves of
the dead," or is Calvin's explanation enlightening:
"those also were in fact baptized who did not expect
to live long, but had death in front of them"? (likewise Bengel). Thus "for the dead" means "who
had death in front of them." A. E. Krauss believes
that Paul meant to ask what was the sense of being
baptized into a community which, if there was no
resurrection, would be a community of the dead on
account of the dangers to which its members would
be exposed. Thus "for the dead" means "in a community of the dead." The most astonishing solution
of this point is found by Hofmann. He joins "for
the dead," instead of with "which are baptized,"
with "what shall they do"; and the first half of the
second sentence, as far as "resurrection," with the
first sentence, understands the "what shall they do
which are baptized" as an independent interrogation; finally, he moves the "for the dead" to the end
of verse 30 and thus obtains the following meaning of verses 29-30: What can the baptized [the
Christians] do for the dead [viz. according to Hofmann here: for the dead in sin] if the dead rise not
at all; what avails them their state of being baptized
[being Christians]? What do even *we* [the preach-
ers of the gospel] rather say to them in every hour
of our lives? The reader will have seen at verses 23
et seq. that I am not insensible to the refinements of
Hofmann's exegesis, and I would gladly assist him

here out of the dilemma, but I do not really think
that this will do. That "the dead" are meant to be
"the dead in sin," and upon this the whole thing
hinges—that alone is, in my estimation, a violent
proceeding which makes it impossible for me to go
thus far, much as I should like to do so. And thus
we have no alternative but to leave the company of
this interpreter and join those led by Erasmus, who
reckon that Paul was here in fact alluding to the
custom of vicarious baptism, which he employed as
a means of proof without arguing against it. The
reader will find a remarkable parallel in Macc. xii.
43-45. Judas Maccabæus offered a sacrifice in Jerusalem for a number of Jews who had fallen in battle,
and at whose burial it transpired that they had
sinned by wearing protective magic tokens: "Doing
therein right well and honourably, in that he took
thought for a resurrection. For if he were not expecting that they that had fallen would rise again,
it were superfluous and idle to pray for the dead."
The Greek world was also acquainted with vicarious
Dionysian orgies for the uninitiated dead, and the
occurrence of Christian vicarious baptism is at least
testified from the circles of Marcionites, Gerinthians,
and Montanists. If we cannot escape from this interpretation, we must explain Paul's opinion in this
wise: You are acquainted with and (from the word-
ing of the sentence the general custom cannot have
been dealt with) some of you have in fact even
practised the custom in question. It does not matter whether it is justifiable (Paul says neither yes
nor no to this); its meaning is the putting not only
of those now living, but of those already dead in con-

nexion, in communion with Jesus Christ. In doing so you affirm the resurrection of the dead, you pass over fundamentally the boundary of human possibilities, which is drawn once for all by death; you acknowledge Jesus Christ as the Lord of Life and Death. Either the custom in question has this meaning, or it has none, or it is only secular, only heathen, only sentimental, like *kerygma*, like "faith," like religion, like being a Christian generally (verses 12-19); it either has this meaning or is "vain." When it is realized from what a fundamentally superior height Paul, throughout this section, surveys and criticizes the whole Christianity of the Corinthians (so far as it is really Christianity, Christian *religion*), we cannot at the end be excessively surprised to see him here taking so seriously such a Greek-Christian border-line possibility in all its ambiguity, as he did the "preaching" and the "faith." Just because it is felt to be repugnant, the combination exerts a rather more penetrating effect in the sense of what Paul means: the super-Christian, as well as the semi- or sub-Christian, is vain and meaningless if the resurrection be not its meaning and substance. I should be the first to rejoice if a more satisfactory explanation of this passage in a credible manner be forthcoming; for the present I see no alternative but to leave the historically insoluble in its mysteriousness, just as we have been obliged to do with regard to Paul's special opinions about marriage in chapter vii. and about the position of women in chapter xi. 7 *et seq.* and about the nature of spiritual gifts in chapters xii. and xiv.

The remaining verses of the paragraph can be

more easily understood. First, verses 30, 32a: "And why stand we in jeopardy?" "We" is the plural frequently used by Paul, by which he means himself, so far as he works and suffers in the discharge of his apostolic office. He calls his life a state of being in jeopardy every hour—in fact, a daily dying. We are reminded of the description which he gives of his existence in 2 Cor. xi. 22 *et seq.* It cannot be sufficiently realized that the Pauline preaching was not only a word uttered above the Cross, but a word uttered beneath the Cross that was continually set up, and thus, *to this extent,* was the Word of the Cross. To be an apostle in the sense of Paul means, *eo ipso,* to jeopardize one's existence not only inwardly, but outwardly. Regarded from the standpoint of life, Paul's existence signifies to him such an impossibility, so much the opposite of life, namely death, that he now includes even himself (after doing so in verse 15 in another sense) within the series of Christian appearances, which without the expectation of the resurrection are sheer absurdities. To be an apostle means to acknowledge life in defiance of death. In defiance of death, and thus in face of death, there where nothing but death is to be perpetually reckoned with, or in that case with the resurrection itself, with the end, or in that case with the entire new beginning itself, but not with that which lies between, only from thence. If this Thence be removed, the apostleship becomes a stupid farce. It would then be really appropriate to discuss the requirements and possibilities of life (of life apart from the Cross) in a somewhat more practical manner.

The sentence of verse 31 is somewhat distorted, and hardly admits of verbal translation: 2 Cor. iv. 12 furnishes the explanatory parallel here: "So then death worketh in us, but life in you." What Paul means is: your glory, your Christianity, with all that it actually is and has, testifies to that fact that I die daily. My oppression unto death is the purchase price of the riches in which you glory and which you now assert against me, against the gospel of the resurrection. But I lay claim to it for myself in Christ Jesus our Lord. What you are and have testifies to what you misconceive and reject. That I, as apostle, can only reckon with death, or then with the resurrection itself, that alone places you in the position, with apparent rightness without fear of death, without faith in resurrection, to regard it differently. But how could I persist in this Either-Or if I were not sure of my cause? if I did not know that the oppression of death must be for the sake of the Life which I preach, which can only be preached from just this standpoint? To take the words "fought with beasts" (verse 32) literally, is not warranted, because this extraordinary incident is mentioned neither in 2 Cor. xi. nor in the Acts of the Apostles, because Paul as a Roman citizen could not be condemned to fight *ad bestias* before he had lost his civic rights, and because the phrase is obviously used as a metaphor. What it rather suggests is the severe and exciting struggles with *human* powers which Paul had to wage at Ephesus. He means that one does not embark upon and wage such struggles after the manner of men. "What advantageth it me?" He who inquires after the profit is too wise to expose himself to such entanglements. The eye for worldly possibilities does not look thither, not even the *diabolicus furor famæ immortalitatis* ("the devilish rage for immortal fame") (Calvin) nor yet the prospect of a blissful death; thence is attracted only the eye for the Kingdom of God, the Kingdom of God ripening unto the eternal harvest, whom I serve, the eye upon the beginning which is set where men reach their end. They see the senseless distorted shape of him who is fighting and suffering; they shake their heads and pass by, and wonder why he takes life so sadly. They are quite right; it *is* indeed senseless to adopt such an attitude towards life if it did not have its meaning in God, in the tidings which he wants to tell the world here; if the task which is here addressed to men is not analogous to the hidden truth of life and, with it, the gift which this man has already received, not in the world, but in eternity.

Verses 32*b*-33 return once more to the Corinthians. They do *not* say: Let us eat and drink; for tomorrow we die. Paul does not quote these words believing that they fit the Corinthians. On the contrary, he addresses them here on their most respectable side; he appeals to the best elements of the Greek world, what might be known to them as the Stoic wisdom of life. They are no Epicureans, no followers of Horace, Eudæmonists. They think they know something of a *law* elevated above all natural fortune and of an *obedience* free from all regard to *desire* and dislike. How much or how little they know of it is not in question; it is enough that they know that *Bios* and *Ethos*, Be and Ought, are not perchance synonymous even for them. They know, even if from a distance, what *pure* authority and *pure* willing are.   But whence in fact? Does not this knowledge testify, is not this knowledge in fact a knowledge of a pure *origin,* of a *whence* of such authority and of a *whither* of such willing, that lie beyond all that is given, all that exists?   If I know only the visible heaven, the heaven in my own breast, the false transcendence which can at any time be converted again into immanence, then I only know a limited authority and a limited willing.   There may be even statues and commandments there—that is, half voluntary, half compulsory conventions—but no eternal law independent of any arbitrariness, and thus also no will directed towards an eternal law.   If we think we know of such within us, even were it merely in the idea, even if it merely consisted in the fact that we could *not* content ourselves with the Horatian wisdom of life, we thereby affirm our membership of the hidden, the coming Kingdom of God.   This knowledge, to be sure, is not to be trifled with: "Be not deceived! evil communications corrupt good manners," quotes Paul from Menander.   He hardly means: the bad company of those who denied the resurrection might corrupt your purity of manners, for there is nothing to indicate that Paul judged the resurrection doubters to be morally inferior, let alone, as Luther used to say, as "swine," "pigheads"; and the boundary between those who denied the resurrection and the rest of the Church is, in my opinion, not to be sharply drawn.   He means: in the environment, in the air of a philosophy, of an attitude towards God and the world, in which the resurrection, in which the fundamental insight into God's being and will made unequivocal by this idea *falls,* the severity of a real authority, of a real will, could *not* thrive. To this environment the phrase "eat and drink" is better suited. In the last resort there is no middle way between real self-denial and the instinctive life of the animal. You must choose sooner or later whether you desire this environment, forgetting that antagonism between *Bios* and *Ethos,* or the other environment, the resurrection and belief in God, which takes its origin from here and receives its nature and, consequently, the practical attitude which you might now at any rate adopt, but which without the latter is as meaningless as every other particle of your Christianity previously discussed.

Hence verse 34, "Become right so far!" "Awake to righteousness and sin not!" Paul sees the Corinthians in an intoxicated or comatose state. Perhaps they were inclined to think the same thing of Paul from the standpoint of their Christianity, bright as the sun and clear as water, and yet, with all its severity and all its depth, life-affirming. Who is more right? This "awake to righteousness," at any rate, shows strikingly that the preaching of the resurrection in the sense of Paul had nothing whatever to do with enthusiasm. Paul was no doubt an enthusiast also, but here, where he spoke his last words, that lay far behind. It was not a question of intuition and enthusiasm, of depth of view or extent of view; no, it was a question of being severely realistic above all towards oneself and

above all towards one's own piety, even if it were
Christianity. The point which falls to be discussed
between Paul and the Corinthians in this section is,
in fact, this: They must realize the relativity of their
Christian religion. Relativity means relationship.
The object of relationship is God, who speaks His
decisive word in the resurrection of the dead, and
upon the existence or non-existence of this relationship hinges the question whether your Christianity
is full of real meaning or is utter nonsense. They
must look upon life as it is. They must ask themselves what the position is with all that they are
and have as Christians, not by way of pretension,
not ideally, not in illusion, but in truth: soap-
bubbles or reality? That means: "to become
sober." And that, and *only that,* is the preliminary
condition of sinning no more, which, indeed, according to verses 17 and 32, they obviously desire to
attain, *then,* sin no more. Otherwise, unsobered,
captivated by the dream of an inner-worldly Christianity, without the hope which is also the *goal,* without the end which is also the *beginning,* you are still
tarrying in your sins. And now come the accusing
—nay, warning—words: "for some have not the
knowledge of God!" We have already discussed
this thoroughly in our survey of the chapter as a
whole. These words should be emblazoned on the
pulpit steps and similar places, so that pastors may
be reminded every time: hence it behoves all of us
now, where possible, not to be ill of this mortal disease of not having the knowledge of God. "To
have no inkling of God!" Some *are* ill of it. Who
are among this some? Who not? But it is really

the mortal sickness of Christianity that perhaps all things are there: correct doctrine, an upright faith, moral earnestness—but with all this not to have knowledge of God—which makes everything vain, empty, and nugatory. "I speak this to your shame." The history of the Church would have run a very different course in many respects if this shaming warning of Paul, with its severity, which is always a little greater than our severity, had been more frequently heeded. Paul has said distinctly enough what is meant. That is the end of the critical section.

§ 3

THE RESURRECTION AS TRUTH (vs. 35-49)

"But some man will say, How are the dead raised up? and with what body do they come?

Thou fool, that which thou sowest is not quickened, except it die:

And that which thou sowest, thou sowest not that body that shall be, but bare grain, it may chance of wheat, or of some other grain:

But God giveth it a body as it hath pleased Him, and to every seed its own body.

All flesh is not the same flesh: but there is one kind of flesh of men, another flesh of beasts, another of fishes, and another of birds.

There are also celestial bodies, and bodies terrestrial: but the glory of the celestial is one, and the glory of the terrestrial is another.

There is one glory of the sun, and another glory of the moon, and another glory of the stars: for one star differeth from another star in glory.

So also is the resurrection of the dead. It is sown in corruption; it is raised in incorruption:
It is sown in dishonour; it is raised in glory: it is sown in weakness; it is raised in power:
It is sown a natural body; it is raised a spiritual body."
—vs. 35-44a.

Fr. Chr. Oetinger has called the chapter I Cor. xv. "a sea of Pauline insights," thinking particularly of the section which we have now reached. He was right enough, and we have every reason to infer from him, from his pupil Bengel, and from the younger J. T. Beck, thus related to them both, that everything which is said here and in similar passages in the Bible is meant in a "real" and not an "ideal" sense. But when Oetinger then proceeds, from the passage just translated, to develop a whole natural philosophy of the resurrecting power of God, which as imperishable seed, as the impelling vital essence, slumbers in every thing, while all else is husk; when he thinks that this can be tested by means of a chemical experiment with oil of balsam, when he and his worthy intellectual colleagues exhibit the general tendency to interpret the truth here represented in the form of a higher natural process, we would listen to them respectfully and attentively, only to say: Be a man and do not follow me! For although, or just because, we are dealing here with nature: a *natural* process, i.e. a process operating with given experiential reality, which might be the subject of perception and experiment, what is here described is emphatically not that. What we are introduced to here is not the "internal processes" of nature which aroused such a burning interest in the eighteenth century, but the *origin* of "nature," its creation and redemption, and the reality here becoming, or rather, not becoming, visible is the reality of which Paul, with the whole Bible, also speaks.

I have chosen the title "The Resurrection as Truth." I might very well have also said: "The conceivability of the resurrection." But that would have been appropriate at the most to verses 35-44*a,* and the sequel 44*b*-49 shows that even these verses have a different meaning, are stronger, more imperative, more absolute. Paul is not philosophizing, he is preaching. He is not exhibiting the truth, that is to say, merely the conceivability of an idea, but he is showing how we ought to think from the standpoint of Christ, of revealed truth. Beyond the whole argument there is already the other thing, which is no longer argument, but only intimation: The resurrection as reality, the conclusion of the chapter, verses 50-58. But for the rest, our section, verses 35-49, has in fact something of a preparatory character. Room is made and the place is designated to which the resurrection belongs. A great disturbing misunderstanding is cleared away and designated. What Paul does here cannot be called apologetics, because the whole chapter is much less a defence of the faith than an attack, not, indeed, upon the world, but, for the sake of the world's salvation, upon Christianity. This is something fundamentally different from apologetics.

But let us now turn to details. The "some man" of verse 35 must not be supposed to be a definite and individual doubter. It is the *objection* to the resurrection that is here referred to. Nor must it even be imagined that this objection was the basis and nerve of the contradiction with which Paul was concerned. It is only the vestment, the conceptual expression, not to say the excuse for an antagonistic Christian-unchristian philosophy. "Those who have no knowledge of God," mentioned in verse 34, base their No, which they openly, or, what is worse, secretly, oppose to the resurrection, upon the fact of the limitation of human knowledge. "How are the dead raised up, and with what body do they come?" (verse 35). What kind of existence is that which, on the one hand, is separated from this known and given existence by death, and, on the other hand, is yet identical with this existence? How can death proceed from life? What kind of a life is that of which, by its definition, we can have no conception? How are we able to affirm the truth of this life? The answer which Paul gives is very exactly articulated.

(1) The general answer: Between the life and death of the same being there is everywhere, if not the resurrection at least the analogon, we might even say the riddle, of the resurrection, between the sown seed and the plant is death! (verse 36). (2) He points to the fact that in nature the same being (*a*) successively (verses 37-38), (*b*) simultaneously (verses 39-41), appears in totally different phenomena without thereby losing its identity. Be it observed that this is not intended to be a description of the resurrection, but an analogy to the resurrection, a *prœludium resurrectionis* ("a prelude to the resurrection"), as Calvin aptly remarks. At the "so also" (verse 42) which makes a metaphor of all the foregoing, the path of a Christian natural philosophy

diverges, in my opinion, from the path which Paul himself takes. (3) The application of the double analogy verses 42-44*a*: As in nature this change of predicate occurs with a persisting subject, so, too, in the resurrection, but is itself no natural process, even of the highest kind, although in nature it has its analogy in the highest as well as in the lowest. Note here: nothing *is*, and nothing can *be*, proved in relation to the resurrection. What is rather shown purely hypothetically is that which the resurrection is, *if* there be a resurrection, so that such questions as the doubters are accustomed to ask may no longer be raised. With more justification than as regards verses 12 *et seq.*, we might here speak of a *petitio principii*. The bringing forward of analogies, and the conclusion drawn from them, point not to something sought, but to something already found.

But let us look at the matter closer. "Thou fool," exclaims Paul (verse 36) to the questioner. Wherein consists the folly of his questioner? The answer is supplied by the following. He does not perceive that in its most primitive process, the growth of a plant from the seed, nature confronts us with the image (only with the image, but no matter, only with the image) of a pure *synthesis*. The grain is alive. Everybody can see that. But what does that mean? We suppose seed and plant to be identical; if we did not do so, if we stopped at what is immediately perceptible: here the seed, there the plant, we should have no image of life as a whole, but only of two chaotic heaps, we should then be really fools, we should then have understood nothing of what will happen to the seed and has happened to the plant.

But in the midst thereof, between the two, lies
somewhere the critical point where the seed, as such,
must die, is transferred and transformed wholly into
the growing plant.   Does this mean perishing?
Surely, but just as surely it means growing!   We
mean this critical point when we regard seed and
plant as identical, although all the predicates of the
seed are here removed, all the predicates of the
plant are here put on, although this change of predicates is still completely inconceivable to us, is, for us,
equivalent to a complete discontinuity.   The zero is
at the same time the synthesis of the *plus* and *minus*
sides.   There is probably no need to read biological
refinements into this.   I am inclined to suppose that
Paul was simply thinking of the earth in whose hidden bosom the change in question is accomplished:
it was seed, it is now plant, without, however, ceas-
ing to be the same.   The subject persists, the predicates have become different.   This is the general
answer which is then taken up in verse 42 and applied.   Verses 37-38 now develop by means of the
same metaphor, the first analogy of the resurrection,
*the change in the appearances of the same thing in
the order of time.*   How are we able to place a necessary continuous connexion between past and future,
between this and that appearance of the same thing,
although the former was obviously something quite
different?   "What thou sowest is not the body which
shall be, but bare grain."   Where was the body of
the plant before, and where is the body of the corn
after?   Answer: in the middle, in the utterly inconceivable critical point between the before and after
lies a creation, more strictly speaking: a new crea-

tion, for something does not come out of nothing
here, but, equally strange, out of Something comes
something different. "God giveth it [the old body]
a [new] body as it hath pleased Him," says Paul.
As before the new body was *not yet,* so now the old
body is *no longer* there. We affirm, as a matter of
course, the identity of old and new, of what is past
and what it has become. To deny that is equivalent
to denying the reality which lies in front of us. But
we affirm, with this identification, not only just
death, as the middle point between the two, but we
affirm the incomprehensible creative life (Paul un-
wittingly makes this equivalent to God, although he
presumably knows that God and creative life are two
things), the One, that in the midst of death changes
into the appearance, in order to prove itself in the
change even more so as the One. By the phrases
"it may chance of wheat, or of some other *grain*"
in verse 37 and "to every seed its own body"
(verse 38), Paul means: this analogy of perishing
followed by growing, in the midst of which a new
creation takes place, penetrates the whole of nature.
Everywhere this enigma is in our midst, whence
alone the perishing and the becoming are to be
understood in their difference and in their oneness,
and yet this itself is as little to be understood as the
present between the past and the future, from which
standpoint alone are both, as such, to be understood.
A fool is he who sees the images and cannot understand them. "Thus," says Luther, "Christians
speak with trees and with all that grows on earth,
and they again with them: for they do not see therein what they are to eat as pigs, but God's word

therein adumbrated, which He will do to us and thus understand this article, to wrap up a precious jewel in a napkin, so as to strengthen and confirm our faith" (*op. cit.* 230 f.). The reference to the variety of the perishing and growing which are yet One is, however, merely the preparation for the second *prœludium resurrectionis* ("preface to the resurrection"), verses 39-42: *the variety of appearances of the same thing in the order of time.* "All flesh *is* not the same flesh." Paul is himself astonished, and designs to excite astonishment in his readers at the fact that a thing (here it is, at any rate, a conception or an idea), can appear successively or simultaneously in various shapes and phenomenal forms. Of this he mentions three examples: Flesh (flesh of man, of beasts, of birds, of fishes), bodies (heavenly and earthly), glory (heavenly and earthly), sun, moon and stars among themselves, everywhere the possibility of change in the appearances of the One, the hypothesis flesh, bodies, glory: and indeed not only of a simple change, but of a three- and fourfold, perhaps even infinite variations, in which the modality and quality of each appearance always signifies the partial or entire abolition of those of their neighbours. It is also a perishing and new becoming which are effected in this change of the predicate: what have heavenly and earthly bodies, for example, to do with each other apart from the One thing that they are both bodies? But because a creative and, to that extent, an *incomprehensible* synthesis is achieved here, only a fool would, for that reason, refuse to comprehend the various things, that is, to grasp them in thought, and therefore to make *use* of this incomprehensible synthesis. The combining of appearances in thought, like that in experience, is an obvious necessity, it is also only an image, but at any rate an image of the resurrection, of the radical, fundamental new-predication of man with the persisting subject.

"So also is the resurrection of the dead" (verse 42). The "so also" indicates a transition to something of a totally different species, the step from the figure to the reality. No proof is adduced, only room is created in thought. We are reminded of the problem of origin with which we are constantly confronted. We must, however, *understand* it. In doing so we have indeed not yet understood God and the resurrection, but *given* the possibility of understanding it if it is to be understood. The resurrection, too, Paul means, is a change, only that here it is man *himself*, the *subject* of all experience, of all thought that changes, who is now to recognize himself in the images of nature and spirit. To be sure, the analogy is not complete, if it were so, the images would, in fact, be superfluous. What in the first analogy was plants, in the second, different flesh, different body, different glory, the second predicate is here obviously *not* given, but *borrowed*. That is to be *understood* here only with the help of and by introducing those analogies. The synthesis, by virtue of which there is a new life here beyond the critical point, must here be first effected. And the analogy is so far complete, but here also an old life is obviously closed by that critical point. The analogies say: there begins the new life. Will this necessity be recognized, will the synthesis be completed?

Paul does not issue this challenge. He only records, "so is it also with the resurrection of the dead," and then, with his "it is sown," reverts to verse 36, where he says that for the sown to be quickened it must die. It ought now to be clear that the meaning is of this dying, the corruptibility, the dishonour, the weakness with which we terminate our life—and not only *terminate* it! That is the darkness of death, undoubtedly the darkness which no light illumines. But if we do not blindly confront the natural and the spiritual world, then it might turn out that we should understand this critical point as the turning point, as the zero which leads from minus to plus. Exactly at this place, at any rate, says Paul, the gospel preaches "incorruption, glory, power," the new predicates of the same subject man "so that all creatures wonder at him, all angels praise and smile upon him, even God Himself will take pleasure in him" (Luther), of the subject man which, however, is now —and with this the resurrection question first becomes really acute—conceived as subject (verse 44a). The corruptibility, dishonour, and weakness of man is, in fact, that of his *corporeality*. Death is the death of his body. If death be not only the end —but the turning point, then the new life must consist in the repredication of his corporeality. To be sown and to rise again must then apply to the *body*. The body is man, body in relation to a non-bodily, determined, indeed, by this non-bodily, but body. The change in the relationship of the body to this non-bodily is just the resurrection. Not, therefore, some transition of man to a merely non-bodily existence. Of such Paul knows nothing whatever. The persisting subject is rather just the body. It is "natural" body this side, "spiritual" body beyond the resurrection. We shall discuss this conception in a moment. *This* re-predication is the "resurrection of the dead." And this antithesis brings us to the logical high-water-mark of the chapter.

"There is a natural body, and there is a spiritual body.

And so it is written, The first man Adam was made a living soul; the last Adam was made a quickening spirit.

Howbeit that was not first which is spiritual, but that which is natural; and afterward that which is spiritual.

The first man is of the earth, earthy: the second man is the Lord from heaven.

As is the earthy, such are they also that are earthy: and as is the heavenly, such are they also that are heavenly.

And as we have borne the image of the earthy, we shall also bear the image of the heavenly."—vs. 44b-49.

"It is sown a natural body; it is raised a spiritual body," states verse 44*a*. In this sentence, Paul has said for the first time quite unequivocally what he understands by the resurrection of the dead, and why he speaks of the resurrection of the dead generally and not, for example, in general terms of the superiority of the creative and redemptive power of God. Without any doubt at all the words "resurrection of the dead" are, for him, nothing else than a paraphrase of the word "God." What else could the Easter gospel be except the gospel become perfectly concrete that God is the Lord? But a *necessary* paraphrase and concretion. God is the Lord! Man might understand by this God's dominion over the *world*, nature, and history, and with this pious

idea just elude God. I am not the world, nature, or
history; if I knew only of this God, I should know
just as little as if I knew only of a fate, I could only
face this God expectantly, unparticipating, gazing.
God is the Lord of *Life*. But man might mean by it
the endless life that *we* know and *its* limitation by
God. In this endless life, however, my life is lost
like a drop of water in the ocean. The conditioning
or limitation of the endless, the universe of things,
by God is certainly a pious idea, but it is equally
certain that it is not an idea which actually and
really lays claim for God on me. God is *Spirit* and
to that extent the Lord. Yes, but from this very
fact man can infer that God is the Lord in *His*
world, a world of Spirit, while we ourselves are left
in our earthly world. God would be our Lord, so far
as we ourselves also shared in the Spirit, so far as we
ourselves are Spirit, but how questionable, at least
how narrow and scanty, to what a fragile relationship our spirituality is restricted, even if its reality
be conceded? But what is the position with regard
to all the rest of our existence, which obviously is
not spirit, but earthy body? God is the Lord of the
body! Now the question of God is posed acutely
and inescapably. Body is man, I am body, and this
man, this I, is God's. But now I have no longer a
refuge from God; I can no longer plead dualism; I
cannot retire to a reality secured against God; I can
no longer make the excuse of earthly weakness. Just
this earthly weakness is meant, if God will be my
Lord. I am this very earthly weak one; I am to be
bound to God, to live in God, to be in glory before
God. The Spirit, not our pinch of spirit and spirit-

uality, but *God's* Spirit triumphs not just in a pure spirituality (*Geistsein*), but: it is raised a (God-) spiritual body, the end of God's way is corporeality. Only with this definition does the idea of God, with which, in fact, Paul is alone concerned, receive that undoubted sublimity, that critical sharpness, that pregnancy with last Judgment and supreme hope, the misunderstanding of which is implied in the very words "have not the knowledge of God" (verse 34).

But this "it is raised a (God-) spiritual body" still remains completely in the air. I would reiterate that verses 35-44*a* do not admit in the least of being interpreted as an attempted biological demonstration of the reality of resurrection. The God-spiritual body, which appears in verse 44*a*, as a result of the whole discussion is not a biological magnitude. It might much rather be called a thanatological magnitude. For if the variety of appearances, seed, plants, and afterwards the flesh of men, of beasts, of birds, etc., is always a variety of the whole, of the *Bios* of natural life, although the contrasts corruptibility-incorruptibility, dishonour-glory, weakness-strength (verses 42-43), could, in case of need, still be conceived as contrasts within this whole, the contrast which at last appears of (human-) natural body and (God-) spiritual body bursts these limits. The spiritual body is something specifically different from, for example, the body that shall be, the plant (verse 37) or the glory of the stars (verse 41). It is not a reality, not something given, that can be perceived or that is possible to be perceived, like all those second things which are cited in these verses by way of contrast to the first ones, as proof of the relative miracle of the changing predication with a persisting substance. The words "it is raised a spiritual body," which appear at the end of this (to be understood as perceptual) trend of thought as the most radical expression of the idea that God is the Lord, constitute the absolute miracle. No way leads *thither*, not even the way of theoretical knowledge, let alone an empirical way. Nature can only offer analogies, similes; the rational contemplation of nature can only make room for the truth of the Resurrection. The Resurrection doubter is a fool (verse 36) only in so far as he fails to understand all those relative things as pointing to the Absolute. If he would confine himself to saying that none of all those relativities is the Absolute, he would in truth be no fool, but that was not the case with the Corinthians, who, in fact, rather fancied they could find the Absolute itself in the world of relative miracle, eternity in time, real life in the presence of God, already in the *natural* body. The "stumbling-blocks" which Paul offered them consisted in the fact that he dared to place the natural body, the tangible, thinking, willing human consciousness in its subjection to the bodily organism in the same category with corruptibility, dishonour, and weakness. In the opinion of the Corinthians the human soul, at least, belonged to the second category, while ignoring, concealing or evading as much as possible the fact that we only know of a soul in connexion with the body. Paul rips this veil. We know only the natural body, at any rate, the human body, but the *body*. And to this body that we know belong corruptibility, dishonour, weakness, together with the soul, or, at least, without the soul altering in any way the character of that which makes it a human body, an organ of spiritual spontaneity, and the body is man, I am the body, and therefore what am I? It is that which Paul obviously aims at impressing upon his readers by means of this offensive combination.

Then comes the further step: "There is a natural body, and there is a spiritual body." I do not believe that the second half of this sentence is to be understood as an inference from the first, as if Paul meant to prove something here, or even intended to assert the *natural* body as a postulate of the *spiritual* body. Consequently, I have translated the Greek *"ei"* not by "if," but by "so far." The reality which Paul announces here follows in no wise from the altogether different reality of the *natural* body. That I am God's, in the concrete sense described, is plainly something New, which is *added* to this fact. Paul's purpose here is not proof, but *description* of the truth of resurrection. Exactly as I am, shall I and will I be God's. Note in passing: the immortality of the soul is placed in dispute by what Paul says here. Instead of the human soul, the Spirit of God appears in the resurrection. That which persists is not the soul (the latter is the predicate, which must give place to something else), but the body, and even that, not as an immortal body, but in the transition from life in death to life. It is not that, however, which Paul wants to indicate here, but the positive aspect. Exactly in the place of that which makes me a man, the human soul, is set that which makes God, God, the Spirit of God, that is the com-

plete sovereignty of God, that is the Resurrection of
the Dead. But exactly in *this* place! To wish to be
God's *without* the body is rebellion against God's
will, is secret denial of God; it is, indeed, the body
which suffers, sins, dies. We are waiting for our
Body's redemption; if the body is not redeemed to
obedience, to health, to life, then there is no God;
then what may be called God does not deserve this
name. The truth of God requires and establishes
the Resurrection of the Dead, the Resurrection of
the Body. But the fact that it does so is not to be
deduced from something else. Paul knows this
already. He does not propose to convince his
readers of this, but *he imparts it to them* as the
unique analogue to the images and similes of which
he was speaking before, "so"—not: it must be so
according to *our* logic, but: it is so, according to
God's order—"it is written." What has Paul seen
written in his Greek Bible, Gen. ii. 2? "God created
man earthy out of the earth and breathed into his
face His breath of life, and man became a living
soul." Paul analyses this text into its constitutent
parts. (1) The Adam, the man who really originated *through the divine breath of life,* is the *second*
Adam, Christ; "the life-giving Spirit" is the predicate of his life, the Spirit, who is not only living for
Himself, but also makes alive that whose Spirit it
is, in other words, the body. What comes from *God's*
breathing upon, the creation in the light of its eternal
origin, this is the very Resurrection of the Dead, the
spiritual body, the new man, who is God's. It is an
utterly immeasurable idea which Paul, in verse 45*b,*
dares to think; the creation, the resurrection of

Christ and the end of all things are here conceived as a single happening: God speaks and the result is His man, the originally finite creature, the Logos become flesh, the last Adam, who is veritably the first.

But of course Paul finds (2) the other as well, which is exegetically more obvious from that text. The Adam who *originated* through the divine breath of life (it must now be emphasized) is the first Adam, the created man, the living soul, the predicate of his body, the soul, which lives for itself, and only for itself, which cannot make living that whose soul it is, in other words, the body. What comes from the breath of God, the creation in the light of *existence*, is just this known, perceiving man, the natural body, the old man, I, so far as I am not God's, but mine own. The knowledge of Christ encompassing all ages *sub specie æterni* corresponds here to the prosaic view of man, who lives in time, who is wholly and exclusively a creature, with all that this, despite the living soul breathed into him, means: corruptibility, dishonour, and weakness. The soul of man is really only the place holder for the divine Spirit of Christ. But Paul has, obviously, also found in this text (3) the man whom *God* creates and man whom God *creates* (the antithesis is best expressed by the change of emphasis), He is not two, but *one*. There exists an indirect identity between the word of God become flesh (compare John i. 14) as was later said, there, and the *creature* here, and it is just corporeality that is the third common thing linking both, and just by it and in it must indirect become direct identity. The truth of God is this, that what really must and will happen to us men is what is stated in verse 44: the change in the predication, which signifies return from creaturehood into primordiality, the reversal from the God-*created* to the *God*-created Adam, the change which is to be effected nowhere else than by and in the palpably visible bodily life of man. That this must *happen,* is now stressed by the following verses, in which Paul, obviously in opposition to the speculations of Philo, but in opposition generally to a misconception which is very obvious here, emphasizes that the *spiritual* body is *not* the first. Logically, in fact, in order to understand verse 45 we could even visualize the spiritual body as the primordial man, as he is in reality as God's work, by virtue of the divine breath of life, the last Adam, in order then, from this standpoint, to understand the *real* man, the unqualified creature, the first Adam. But this would too readily lend itself to being understood as a modification of idea and appearance, and the resurrection would then too easily be understood as a mere relation, somewhat in the manner of a mathematical functional relationship. Paul, however, means something more urgent, something more actual, something more aggressive by this antithesis and consequently he reverses the ideas of Philo: *Adam* the *first, Christ* the second man. In this way, he will avoid its appearing as if the reality of the new man should lie behind us like a lost paradise, like a Platonic idea, as it seems according to the common understanding of Plato, a truth which is only in heaven, but never *our* truth, or our truth *only* in heaven. No, it becomes *our* truth, not by our undertaking the hopeless task of going to heaven, but *by its coming to us from heaven*. Christ *before* us, coming, in future, eternity no general given truth! How dreadful, if we have to tell ourselves, that it is already given for us, and that the scanty thing we are now and have is already the life of the new man, so that we should already have our reward there! No, what we now are and what we have is fortunately only the First, and as such, at least, fixed and given with decisive precision: the first man from the earth, earthy. We may always honestly start from the point that this may not be cloaked and embellished. We are from below—even the living soul we know only as an earthly magnitude, living, but standing and falling with our standing and falling body. For Adam is not alone. This "earthly clod" is followed by earthly clods (verse 48); we have borne *his* image (verse 49). But this past comprises the whole of time. Confronting it stands, indeed, as the future "we shall bear, etc." But between past and future lies the resurrection. Do not let us deceive ourselves as if the time has already gone; we all are the first Adam. So far as we are existing in a historical connexion here and now, he is *this* connexion. So far as we are realizing an idea in our existence here and now, it is the idea of the *human being* with the living soul. So far as we are permitted to appeal to God's creation and its orders here and now, it is just the created creation, the temporal man, the orders under which he must in fact exist so long and so far as he is man with a soul and not with the Spirit of God, and Paul did not believe so confidently in the existence of really "pneumatic" persons as the Corinthians, who thought they saw and recognized one or other of them at every street corner and on every church bench. No, *"then,"* the spiritual body (verse 46), the real "pneumatic," the second man is the Lord from heaven (verse 47) which is, however, for us always the non-given, that which is only given from God, the *absolute* miracle. Here we can only believe, not see. But we can believe Him. He is our hope, because He is from above. "And in hope we are saved." For it also applies here: as is the heavenly, such are they also that are heavenly. We shall bear His image. The future tense tells us that we (*the* heavenly) are not to confuse ourselves with the heavenly man. Men of the Spirit here and now are a contradiction in terms. We all lapse into psychology with that which we would pride ourselves upon as spiritual possessions. Between us and Christ exists no continuity. Only the relationship of hope. But the relationship of hope *exists:* "we *shall* bear." The reading of "let us bear," conjunctive, which makes the sentence a summons, is certainly as false as the reading of Rom. v. 1 ("Being therefore justified by faith, we have peace," but not "let us have peace.") Both derive from the moralizing tendency of a later time, which no longer understood such an apostolic indicative mood. *Non est exhortatio sed pura doctrina*—"this is not moral exhortation but pure teaching" (touching a matter of fact), Calvin very justly observes. And it is more than a mathematical function, however certainly it admits of no better description than the helpless expression "indirect identity." We thus stand in the connexion of *salvation history,* which is a real history: the perishing of an old, the becoming of a new, a path and a step on this path, no mere relationship, but history which is not enacted in time, but between time and eternity—*the* history, in which the creation, the resurrection of Christ, and the End, as verse 48 indicates, are one day. We realize even the idea of man with the life-giving Spirit of God, but in the coming of *Christ*. We can and may appeal to the primordial, to the redeemed *creation,* and hence to no existing thing, to no given thing; hence to the orders which are only to be understood as coming from above. So, therefore, Paul preached the truth of the resurrection. In reply to the question, How? (verse 35), he points to the *So,* which is at least reflected in the growth and decay, in the being so and the being different, of visible things. And thus he places man forcibly in the light, or, rather, twilight, of the truth that he is created by God in the middle between Adam and Christ, and tells him: Thou art *Both,* or rather thou *belongest* to both, and just as both jointly describe God's way, from the old to the new creature, so thy life also is the scene across which this path leads, so must thou, too, make the journey *from* here *to* there. In other words, he jerks the questioner and spectator out of his comfortable position and sets him right in the midst of the *struggle,* in which the resurrection is truth. He who recognizes himself in Adam and Christ no longer, in fact, asks: With what body shall we come again? as if it were a marvellous fairy-tale which he must "believe." He knows that what is in question is *this,* his body (but the *resurrection* of this body), and gives God the honour in fear and trembling, but also in hope. Not in the theory, but only in the practice of this struggle, is it to be understood: the Resurrection as *truth*, but here it *is* to be understood.

§ 4

THE RESURRECTION AS REALITY

"Now this I say, brethren, that flesh and blood cannot inherit the Kingdom of God; neither doth corruption inherit incorruption. Behold, I show you a mystery. We shall not all sleep, but we shall all be changed. In a moment, in the twinkling of an eye, at the last trump: for the trumpet shall sound, and the dead shall be raised incorruptible, and we shall be changed. For this corruptible must put on incorruption, and this mortal must put on immortality. So when this corruptible shall have put on incorruption, and this mortal shall have put on immortality, then shall be brought to pass that saying that is written, 'Death is swallowed up in victory.' O death, where is thy sting? O grave, where is thy victory? The sting of death is sin; and the strength of sin is the law. But thanks be to God, which giveth us the victory through our Lord Jesus Christ. Therefore, my beloved brethren, be ye stedfast, unmoveable, always abounding in the work of the Lord, forasmuch as ye know that your labour is not in vain in the Lord."—vs. 50-58.

What remains to be said now after all that has already been said, and in view of the fact that all words fail before the point which is now almost within our reach? The title which I have given to this chapter must not be understood to imply that something will now be said which has not previously been adumbrated. With the exception, perhaps, of verses 51-52, that is not the case, and even there we have to do more with a new explanation than with a new thesis. No, the new thing in this last section compared with the preceding I would fain simply see in the calm way in which Paul now no longer disputes publicly (verse 50 is at least only a definite summary of the whole antithesis, but its effect here is no longer argumentative, however weighty its critical substance), not even by way of instructing in the knowledge of truth, but now (this was also the case from verse 44*b* in the preceding section) simply proceeds from the resurrection as reality, and testifies to it for what it is. Why is? Yes, why? Could Paul himself make any different answer than: because God is and because He has revealed Himself? To say anything more than this as an apostle and as a man who could say "He was also seen of me" (verse 8) Paul had not, in fact, promised. In the first section of our chapter he recalled not his theology and its art, but the gospel that stands above his theology. In the second chapter he subjected Corinthian Christianity to that sharp criticism, not from a sophisticated standpoint, but from an ultimately very simple standpoint, which could be understood by a child. And, as we saw, even in the third section he adduced no proof, and only directed attention to figures of speech. Then in the decisive moment the figures fail, and he can only say that we are men of Adam and are to become men of Christ as *corporeal* men, else it would *not* be true, but as a *quite different* corporeal man, otherwise it would *also* not be true. And thus the last section must now be understood as simply halting in front of the attained goal.

A number of explanatory remarks have still to be made, a misunderstanding cleared away (verses 50-53), and then, in a concluding word (verses 54 *et seq.*) which is more of a psalm than a continuation of the lecture, to be compared, say, with Rom. viii. 31-38 or Rom. xi. 32-36, it is established: this is just the glorious reality before which we as Christians stand, and which (but this is no longer expressly added) ought not to be forgotten or in any way denied. Verse 58, with its quite calm and friendly tone, abstaining from any more remote criticism, indicates that Paul has now quite descended the high mountain which he had climbed. He has now to give one more strong exhortation, yet full of promise and entirely constructive, to those whose communion with him at the level of the preceding discussions seemed in truth more than once to be much endangered.   Observe also the perfectly human objectivity of the almost purely "business" chapter xvi., in which only a last, short glimpse (xvi. 22 *et seq.*) recalls what has gone before.   This, then, is the way in which we can talk to each other, touching lightly upon the most difficult "uprooting" errors and misunderstandings, when we are really talking about the *resurrection of the dead.*   In truth, it is this calm tone of the witness, with all his animation, which makes the last section of our chapter so weighty and impressive.

Let us now turn to the details.   Reference has already been made in a previous place to the fundamental significance of verse 50.   Here we have the theme of the entire chapter before us, so far, indeed, as it is a critical and polemical chapter. It is quite clear that these two sentences do not admit of being utilized, as occasionally happens, *against* the idea of bodily resurrection. Those who do so have wrongly understood the meaning of the whole third section, and come most sharply into conflict with verses 53 *et seq.*, where, by means of the word "this," which occurs four times, it is said distinctly enough that Paul means the body, and, indeed, *this* body, when he sets man in the light of his last great hope. But that is the very thing which Paul's contradictors do not yet see: this man—that is to say, this *body* as such—*without* this last hope is definitely and entirely outside the Kingdom of God. Within this life of the body as such there exists no possibility of inheriting the Kingdom, to do which one must be the Son coming from heaven, the Lord from heaven (verses 47 *et seq.*), or one of his own (in the future resurrection). We must mentally insert after the words "flesh and blood" in verse 50 the words "in itself" or "here and now" or "in time" or "intuitively," and then everything becomes clear. Paul asserts the identity of this perishable and mortal body (verses 53-54) with the *spiritual* body, with the man who is God's. But this identity is not given. Between it and the *natural body,* that which we *know* as "*flesh and* blood," is the miracle of God, the most severe, the most destructive judgment and the hope that is unique. It is that which is not understood in Corinth. God is not understood there, that is to say, as the beginning, as the foundation, as the vital *secret,* never to be taken as self-understood, of

this identity. To live means not to be as such in the
Kingdom of God, although it be a Christian life.
But now it behoves us to pay attention to the sequel.
Paul adds, and obviously means, a *second:* neither
the *dead*, neither doth corruption inherit incorruption: it is an equally great error to think that by
dying in itself one becomes immortal. Life and
death rather approximate, faced with the reality of
the resurrection. Flesh and blood do not create it,
neither does the death of flesh and blood create it,
although, as need not be said, Paul undoubtedly
saw in death the door to the true life. Once more
must the miracle of God step in between corruption
and incorruption, so that the latter may inherit the
former. Also the dying, the dead man, as much and
as little as the living man, is the *unredeemed* man.
This Yes and No, that I am living or that I am dead,
the life of my body or its dissolution, is in reality *not
yet the* Yes and No that God speaks to me, the life
that *He* wills me to live and the death that He wills
me to die. That is *not yet* the resurrection of the
dead. But what then? "Behold I show you a mystery" (verse 51). The mystery which Paul here
discloses is (if we have understood what has gone
before we shall not be altogether surprised at it) *the
synchronism of the living and the dead in the resurrection.* "We shall not all sleep"—that is, in order
to participate in the resurrection. To be sure, it
touches the greater part of men, from our point of
view, as the dead, but whether dead or living, we
shall all be changed. The resurrection, the crisis
which concerns all men in all ages, means, as surely
as it is God's decisive word to mankind: "In Him

they *all* live." The ribbon of time which, to our eyes, is unwound endlessly, is in God's view rolled up into a ball, a thousand years as a day. Together He calls Abraham and us and our children's children. That *He calls* is what decides the reality of the resurrection, not that we live, and not that we die. Rom. xiv. 8 and its conclusion may be recalled: "Whether we live and whether we die, we are the *Lord's*." Just as even also Christ is the second Adam, as the embodiment of the life-giving Spirit, the beginning and the end. (The same "synchronism," 1 Thess. iv. 13-17.)

Verse 52 mentions three remarkable symptoms of this dawning crisis which rips up all ages lengthwise: First, it will happen literally "in a moment," therefore not even in a fraction of time, else it could not happen at any rate to all races simultaneously, but in the *present*. Only the present is really a moment between past and future. Secondly: "in the twinkling of an eye"; which is perhaps intended to describe the "suddenness" of the dawning of this crisis. It does not come in gradual or catastrophical developments; if such happen, they have nothing to do with it: the resurrection cuts clean through the life and death of man, it is salvation-history which cleaves its own way through the other histories. Thirdly: "at the sound of the last trump." This is the decisive sign of this crisis. God *wills* it (the trumpet is the sign of command; astounding things about this trumpet—the "tara-tantara"—may be read in Luther), not indeed only by way of preliminary, but finally; not only by way of warning and preparation, but urging with His whole author-

ity immediate departure and obedience. When that
shall happen, when the last trump "shall" sound
(do not for a moment forget to put this "shall" in
quotation marks, it relates to this quite special
Futurum resurrectionis or *æternum!*), then "shall"
both meet their fate. The dead shall awake, we,
the living, be changed. The meaning might equally
well be expressed by saying: we shall all be awakened, except that, applied to the living, this would
sound harsh. What *resurrection* and what *change*
mean is explained by verse 53: what the dead and
the living have to do is to put on incorruption and
immortality. Where they are to be found, and how
men will be able to put on such a garment, is shown
by a glance at verses 44*b*-49: because they have
Adam behind them and Christ before them, here the
old, there the new man; the one, the sign of what
they are, the other, the sign of what they are to become. The resurrection, it is here said positively,
is absolutely in the power of God, when the pneumatic body that is now hidden becomes visible and
the "psychic," natural body now visible becomes hidden, because it will be clothed upon by the latter
(2 Cor. v. 1 *et seq.*)—*then* (we interpret: *from this
standpoint,* in this truth of God) is "Christianity"
truth, with its claim, with its victorious tidings,
"Death is swallowed up in victory" (verse 55).
Apart from this all-changing "then," applied to our
now and here, *without* this secret reversal of all
things, Christianity is not truth, and the word of
promise could not be taken seriously. It needs the
miracle of God, which sets man's goal definitely before him, so that even all-embracing death is com-

manded to halt. From this standpoint death can
and must be mocked. This last, seen from every
angle *this side,* is and remains the victor, to whom
there can be no resistance, the bearer of the *"ken-
tron"* (poisonous sting?) from whom there is *no*
escape. "Death" means the dualism *not yet* overcome of "Life and Death," the endlessness of the
irreversible time series, deprived of all present, the
unabolished mere humanity of our existence. We
know what the "reality of the resurrection" holds
out (verse 56), what *separates* us from the "then"
of verse 54, what forbids and prevents us from forthwith (monistically) placing ourselves there, from
anticipating the word of promise as if we were already living from "thence": *sin* is the "sting" of
death. Because as children of Adam we participate with our existence in his *fall,* in his *rebellion*
against God, because not only our existence, but
primarily our will, the will which we assert ourselves
in our distinction from God (Rom. v. 12 *et seq.*),
because our life as our *act* (not merely as our fate!)
establishes the dualism, for this reason death triumphs, for this reason its sting strikes, for this reason *we do not* stand in the centre of indifference
above "life" and "death." The "power" of sin
consists, however, in the fact that (Rom. vii. 7
et seq.) it has seized hold of our divine relationship,
just the holy, just, good *God*-confrontation of man,
the law; making him commit a transgression just
here on the summit of his humanity, "working death
in me by that which is good" (Rom. vii. 13). Because it is *thus within* our existence, even our Christian existence, and always must be, however high we

climb, because the "then" is really a *Then* and *There*, no Now and Here, the *reality* of the resurrection is exclusively the reality of the *resurrection*, the truth of Christianity is exclusively *God's* truth, its absoluteness is exclusively *God's* absoluteness. What remains to *us*, what falls to us? (verse 57). "Thanks be to God" (exact parallel to Rom. vii. 25).

"Faith is *weak*, wilts under God's *judgment*, seizes the proffered umbrella of *hope*, of salvation, and shows everywhere that it is more concerned about *God, His* honour, the holiness of *His* name, the fulfilment of *His* work, and that it is enough for us that God has so faithfully interwoven our salvation with this *His* honour" (C. H. Rieger). Through "our Lord Jesus Christ" God *gives* us the victory. Note the present tense: "which *giveth* the victory"! As *God's gift*, the victory, the "reality of the resurrection," is *present;* is valid word spoken to us, not to be forgotten, not to be dragged down into the dialectic of *our* existence, not to be restricted, not to be weakened, not to be doubted. But just for this reason everything depends upon this "victory" being and remaining God's gift "through our Lord Jesus Christ" present in *hope*. There is no presence of God fuller, more joyful and stronger than that in the eternal future; there is no having, possessing, and enjoying more real than in the words spoken with empty hands: "But thanks be to God," in which *all* right and *all* glory is given to Him with whom that which falls to us is abolished. *"Therefore,* my beloved brethren (verse 58), *thus* and *therein* be ye stedfast, unmoveable, always abounding in the work of the Lord." As certain as it is that "if the hope of the resurrection be removed, the whole edifice of piety would collapse, just as if the foundation were withdrawn from it" (Calvin), just as certain is the other thing, that, once the reality of the resurrection, and in it the reality of God, is recognized, man can and may tread the so infinitely narrow path, the knife-edge of Christianity. "He who has descended from the holy mountain where God holds intercourse with men, retains a reflection of the light which lights up even the dark valleys" (A. E. Krauss). Or, expressed in other words: "He who has become acquainted with sin and grace, death and life, and preserved in himself the roots of eternal life through the knowledge of our Lord Jesus Christ, may stand fast against the inner inconstancy of the heart and the senses, be immovable against outward temptations, escape peevish fatigue, ever increasing rather in the works of the Lord, of which faith is the driving-wheel to everything else" (C. H. Rieger).

The tension in which the thoughts of Paul move is unprecedented. I do not think I have exaggerated it; I fear rather the contrary. It is not tension of a successive order, but tension of an intertwining character. Just because of this it is an irremovable *real* tension, a "stumbling-block" to the understanding of the wise and a folly unto them that are called (cf. i. 24). It is the tension of *faith*. If it seems unbearable to anyone, he should ask himself how the tensions of human life, of which we know more to-day than in other ages, are to be encountered except with the yet greater tension of faith. Pauline theology, Pauline Christianity with its word of the resurrection in the centre, shows it to us. We have *everything* to learn in this school. That centre is not a matter about which we should always be talking—Paul himself did not do so—but we should always be *thinking* of it.

Printed in the United States of America

THE LITERATURE OF
DEATH AND DYING

Abrahamsson, Hans. **The Origin of Death:** Studies in African Mythology. 1951

Alden, Timothy. **A Collection of American Epitaphs and Inscriptions with Occasional Notes.** Five vols. in two. 1814

Austin, Mary. **Experiences Facing Death.** 1931

Bacon, Francis. **The Historie of Life and Death with Observations Naturall and Experimentall for the Prolongation of Life.** 1638

Barth, Karl. **The Resurrection of the Dead.** 1933

Bataille, Georges. **Death and Sensuality:** A Study of Eroticism and the Taboo. 1962

Bichat, [Marie François] Xavier. **Physiological Researches on Life and Death.** 1827

Browne, Thomas. **Hydriotaphia.** 1927

Carrington, Hereward. **Death:** Its Causes and Phenomena with Special Reference to Immortality. 1921

Comper, Frances M. M., editor. **The Book of the Craft of Dying and Other Early English Tracts Concerning Death.** 1917

Death and the Visual Arts. 1976

Death as a Speculative Theme in Religious, Scientific, and Social Thought. 1976

Donne, John. **Biathanatos.** 1930

Farber, Maurice L. **Theory of Suicide.** 1968

Fechner, Gustav Theodor. **The Little Book of Life After Death.** 1904

Frazer, James George. **The Fear of the Dead in Primitive Religion.** Three vols. in one. 1933/1934/1936

Fulton, Robert. **A Bibliography on Death, Grief and Bereavement:** 1845-1975. 1976

Gorer, Geoffrey. **Death, Grief, and Mourning.** 1965

Gruman, Gerald J. **A History of Ideas About the Prolongation of Life.** 1966

Henry, Andrew F. and James F. Short, Jr. **Suicide and Homicide.** 1954

Howells, W[illiam] D[ean], et al. **In After Days;** Thoughts on the Future Life. 1910

Irion, Paul E. **The Funeral:** Vestige or Value? 1966

Landsberg, Paul-Louis. **The Experience of Death:** The Moral Problem of Suicide. 1953

Maeterlinck, Maurice. **Before the Great Silence.** 1937

Maeterlinck, Maurice. **Death.** 1912

Metchnikoff, Élie. **The Nature of Man:** Studies in Optimistic Philosophy. 1910

Metchnikoff, Élie. **The Prolongation of Life:** Optimistic Studies. 1908

Munk, William. **Euthanasia.** 1887

Osler, William. **Science and Immortality.** 1904

Return to Life: Two Imaginings of the Lazarus Theme. 1976

Stephens, C[harles] A[sbury]. **Natural Salvation:** The Message of Science. 1905

Sulzberger, Cyrus. **My Brother Death.** 1961

Taylor, Jeremy. **The Rule and Exercises of Holy Dying.** 1819

Walker, G[eorge] A[lfred]. **Gatherings from Graveyards.** 1839

Warthin, Aldred Scott. **The Physician of the Dance of Death.** 1931

Whiter, Walter. **Dissertation on the Disorder of Death.** 1819

Whyte, Florence. **The Dance of Death in Spain and Catalonia.** 1931

Wolfenstein, Martha. **Disaster:** A Psychological Essay. 1957

Worcester, Alfred. **The Care of the Aged, the Dying, and the Dead.** 1950

Zandee, J[an]. **Death as an Enemy According to Ancient Egyptian Conceptions.** 1960